MW01139544

DEADLY FIRES

Strong Women, Extraordinary Situations
Book Nine

Margaret Daley

Deadly Fires
Copyright © 2017 by Margaret Daley

All rights reserved. No part of this book may be reproduced in any form or by any electronic or mechanical means, including information storage and retrieval systems, without permission in writing from the author, except by a reviewer, who may quote brief passages in a review.

All texts contained within this document are a work of fiction. Any resemblance to actual events, locales or persons (living or dead), is entirely coincidental.

Strong Women, Extraordinary Situations Series

Deadly Hunt, Book 1

Deadly Intent, Book 2

Deadly Holiday, Book 3

Deadly Countdown, Book 4

Deadly Noel, Book 5

Deadly Dose, Book 6

Deadly Legacy, Book 7

Deadly Night, Silent Night, Book 8

Deadly Fires, Book 9

Deadly Secrets, Book 10

ONE

Alexia Richards sat in a chair behind a desk she was using temporarily, wishing she could wipe away the last couple of hours. But she couldn't. Tension lassoed her and wouldn't let go. Her chance to prove herself to her father was disappearing faster than a wisp of smoke in a brisk wind. Before she called the company's insurance agent, she closed her eyes and drew in deep breaths.

Maybe her dad wouldn't hear about the incident. The family ranch was three hours away in central Montana.

The blare of the phone ringing jerked her straight up in the chair. She looked at the caller ID number and couldn't believe how fast the word spread that Bulldog, a top rated, two-thousand-pound rodeo bull, had escaped from his pen and terrified a young family, holding them hostage in their car.

She picked up the receiver.

"What have you done, Alex? First, money went missing from petty cash at the last venue and now this!" Her father's outburst quelled her hello.

She could picture her dad pacing, his face red with anger at her for letting him down—yet again. "I did nothing. Someone let Bulldog out of his pen."

"Who?"

"I don't know. The police—"

"What have they done to find the person who stole from us? Nothing!"

No doubt his blood pressure was off the charts. Where was Mom? She was supposed to keep him away from the family business while recovering. "Dad, calm down. I'm taking care of this. Remember you just had a massive heart attack and—"

"I'm calling the Knight Investigation

Agency."

At the mention of the agency, she sucked in a deep breath and held it.

"If anyone can get to the bottom of this, Michael can."

Relief flooded her. Michael. She could deal with him but not Cole. For a brief moment, she imagined her ex-husband the last time she'd seen him in his U.S. Army uniform leaving the courtroom, their divorce finalized. She'd heard rumors he was back in Montana and working for Michael after being honorably discharged from the army, but she didn't know for sure.

Before her thoughts fixed on why they had divorced, her father continued, "Expect a visit from Michael. Better yet, I think you two should meet here at the ranch house. I need to sit in on the meeting."

Left unsaid—*so I can make sure the incidents are stopped for good*. "Dad, Mom made you promise not to work for at least six weeks. It's only been two weeks since you came home from the hospital. Besides, the Crescent City Rodeo's tomorrow. I need to be here." Not on the road driving for hours. She could never make it to the Flying Red Ranch and back in time for the performance at the Crescent City's Founders' Day Celebration.

He harrumphed. "You'd better give me a detailed report in person right after."

"I'll keep you—"

"I'll have Michael come see you tomorrow morning. Then he can come see me. Bye."

The phone went dead, leaving her holding the receiver to her ear for a few extra seconds as she tried to assimilate being rolled over by a bulldozer. Why was she working for the Red Richards Rodeo Company?

Because I wanted to be the son my dad never had. Because family is important to me. But lately, nothing she did satisfied him. It was never enough. Even with his health issues, he was breathing down her neck and questioning every move she made. She would meet with Michael, but no way would she be informing her father in person. She had a show to oversee

4

tomorrow.

When the phone rang a second time, the sound startled Alexia again, and she quickly answered the call, hoping it was the police with good news. "Red Richards Rodeo Company. How can I help you?"

"Alexia, this is Michael Knight. I got a call from Red about a problem you're having in Crescent City with your show. He started to explain when your mother interrupted the call and told me to talk with you about it."

She smiled. Her mother was the only one who could handle her dad. Mom had been the one who pushed to have her fill in for her dad while he was recuperating. "We had three shows in the past six days. In the third town, someone must have broken into the office we were using the night of our performance. The next morning, when I went to pack up the office, the money in the petty cash box was gone. Thankfully, only a couple of hundred dollars." She went on to explain about the incident with Bulldog. "Mr. Davis, the father of the family trapped in the car, was understanding. I've invited them to be our guests at the show. His young son is thrilled he gets to be part of the opening event."

"It sounds like you handled it diplomatically. Any damage?"

"Bulldog left a couple of dents in their car."

"I know that bull's reputation. You're lucky it wasn't worse."

"His reputation is what draws the crowds to our shows. These two events may not be connected. They were in two different towns, four hours away from each other."

A long pause ensued before Michael asked, "When are you leaving Crescent City?"

"Thursday. We have one more venue to go before we return to the ranch."

"Good. I'll be there early in the morning."

"How's Bella doing?" She'd been so glad when Michael married Bella two years ago. He deserved a happily ever after.

"Fine. She can't wait until the baby comes next month."

"I heard through the grapevine you two are having a boy."

"Yes."

"Tell her I said hi, and I've already found the perfect baby gift."

"I will."

When Michael hung up, Alexia sank back against the hard slats of the desk chair. She'd worked for the family company since she was twelve, mostly as a performer—a trick rider until she married Michael's cousin, Cole Knight, six years ago. A year later she became pregnant. By that time, Cole was stationed in Georgia where his unit was based, although they deployed worldwide. She moved there, but over half the time, Cole was gone on secret missions he could never talk about. Her life revolved around her child and the brief times Cole was home.

Memories of her own child inundated her. Her son, Daniel, died three years ago, leaving an emptiness in her life she didn't think would ever be filled. Since the fire that took his life, a coldness embedded itself into her heart, and she'd gone through the motions of living but the joy was gone. The only thing she had was her job, which, at times like this, she questioned doing. When she moved back to Montana after her divorce, she'd agreed to become her father's assistant because her mother had begged her to help take some of the pressure off him. But he couldn't let go even when he came down with the shingles and the flu last year. Although her mother had tried to get him to cut back, he'd still worked twelve or fourteen hours a day, even sick, until his heart attack and recent near death.

She had to admit her demanding job had kept her sane after her life had been turned upside down. During the day, she could manage not to think of Daniel, but not always at night. Dreams of the fire dominated her memory, leaving her exhausted in the morning as she fought her demons.

She was the reason her child was dead, and she'd never forget that—or forgive herself.

* * *

In the dim light of dawn, Cole Knight fumbled for his cell phone on his nightstand, glanced at the caller ID, and asked, "What's up, Michael?"

"I need you to take over a case this morning. I know you just returned from working one in Wyoming, but Bella's going into labor four weeks early. I'm driving her to the hospital right now. I can't make the meeting in Crescent City."

Cole rolled to an upright position, his muscles protesting along with his sleep-deprived mind. "There isn't anyone else who can do it? I only got back at three this morning."

"No, not in the area, and you're even closer to Crescent City than I am. Even if this is a false alarm, I can't leave Bella."

"Who is it?" Shaking the cobwebs from his mind, Cole sat on the side of the bed.

There was a long pause on Michael's end.

"Is something wrong?" Cole asked, remembering the time he'd had to rush

9

Alexia to the hospital, only ending up having to deliver his own son. A knot jammed his throat. He closed his eyes, trying to stop the onslaught of memories.

"Someone's stolen petty cash and let a bull out to run loose in Crescent City."

Another pause alerted Cole something was wrong.

"Who will I be working for?"

"The Red Richards Rodeo Company. I know you and Red used to be close—"

"I heard he had a heart attack. Did I hear wrong?"

"No, and the person you'll be working with isn't Red but Alexia."

"That's not a good idea." He couldn't shake the last time he'd seen her in the courtroom. He'd been halfway around the world when their son died. He'd let her down when she'd needed him the most, and there wasn't any way he could fix that.

"I wouldn't have asked if I had another option. I've gotta go. I'm at the hospital."

Cole's grip on his cell phone tightened until every muscle in his right arm tensed. "Don't worry. I'll take care of the situation."

Somehow.

"Thanks. I'll let you know what happens here."

When Michael ended the call, Cole tossed his phone on his bed then shoved to his feet. He would need to hustle to get to Crescent City in time. After a quick, cold shower, he dressed, grabbed a protein bar and a large cup of coffee then hopped into his truck.

He hadn't returned to Montana until six months ago when he accepted a job working for the Knight Investigation Agency, which specialized in cases involving the rodeo and ranching business. He'd grown up not far from Michael, Sean, and Jesse's family ranch. They were first cousins but also good friends. He'd followed Jesse into the armed forces but had served in a different branch. He'd become a member of the U.S. Army's Delta Force while Jesse had been a U.S. Marine. Neither talked much about their time serving their country. He didn't think he could put into words his thoughts and memories of his service as a soldier. He'd discovered blocking those memories from his thoughts, as he did the death of his son, was the only way he survived to do what he must.

But now he wouldn't be able to block Alexia and Daniel from his mind.

What are you telling me, God?

To forget and forgive the past?

He didn't know if he could.

He slammed shut the door on his past the closer he came to Crescent City. Did Michael tell Alexia he would be taking his place? He should have asked, but he hadn't been thinking this morning when his cousin called.

As he arrived in Crescent City, he spotted a fast food chain known for their coffee. He swung across a lane of traffic to pull into their drive-thru then ordered the largest cup and pulled back onto the main road that led to the city park and the rodeo grounds. When he parked in front of the building that housed the facility's offices, he finished his drink then sat and drummed his fingers against the steering wheel. His stomach churned as though the coffee hadn't agreed with him for the first time ever. He lived on it most days.

He closed his eyes and said another silent prayer for help to handle meeting Alexia. He hadn't seen her in three years. A vision of her in the courtroom, sitting next to her lawyer, avoiding eye contact with him, filled his mind. The haunted look in her big brown eyes and an ashen sheen to her pale creamy complexion roiled his gut even more.

Remembering only made the situation worse. *Get in and get out safely*. On his assignments with his Delta Force team, those words had become his mantra.

He shoved the driver's door open and climbed down from the cab.

When he entered the building, he hadn't prepared himself enough for seeing her again. Alexia stood at the end of the long corridor, talking to a police officer, her usual loose long brown hair pulled back in a tight bun.

She turned toward Cole, and their gazes clashed.

* * *

Alexia froze at the sight of her ex-husband only fifteen feet away. His stare drilled through her, challenging her to look away. She didn't.

Why was he here now? Bad timing—unless Michael sent him. If that was the case, she didn't want his help, especially with all that was happening. She'd needed it three years ago. He was too late.

Alexia turned away from him and shifted more toward the police officer. "The only surveillance camera that picked up the person who let Bulldog out of his pen doesn't really help to ID the culprit?"

"Yes, ma'am. The man's about five feet ten inches to six feet. He wore baggy clothes, and he was hunched over with a hoodie covering his face. He walked funny. And that's the only camera that showed anything. One camera was disabled. Another never worked. They kept it there only for show."

"Thanks, Officer Cassidy. Please let me know if anything else develops."

He nodded. "I will."

While the police officer left, Alexia hurried into her temporary office, considering slamming the door and locking it before Cole appeared. But she knew that was futile. He was a very determined man. Working for the Knight Investigation Agency was a good job choice for Cole. She just wished it wasn't this case.

She managed to get behind her desk before he came into the office. His presence seemed to fill the whole room. Nothing had changed. As the warrior he was for ten years, he radiated self-assurance and command.

"Why didn't Michael come?" she asked before Cole said anything.

"Bella went into labor early."

Oh, no. She knew how much Michael and his wife wanted a child. "Is everything okay?"

"I haven't heard from Michael yet."

"Are you only filling in for today?"

"No. Michael said if it was false labor, he still felt he needed to stay with Bella." Cole sat in a chair in front of the desk.

She'd practically gone through raising their baby alone in Georgia. And even worse, the first week after their son had died in a fire, Cole had been away on a top-secret assignment, leaving her to deal with Daniel's death by herself. Even when Cole had arrived home, his mind was somewhere else. "That's where Michael should be." Alexia sat before she collapsed into the chair behind her. She'd hardly slept the night before, wondering what would occur next to the rodeo company.

"Did something else happen since yesterday?"

"No. Officer Cassidy was letting me know about the footage from the cameras in the area of Bulldog's pen. Unfortunately, there's nothing to help the police other than the vague height of the guy: five ten to six feet—and even that was a conjecture."

"I'll talk with Officer Cassidy and see if I can get a look at the tape. Another pair of eyes on it might help." He took a pad out of his coat pocket and wrote on it. "Give me the details concerning Bulldog's release."

16

"A worker notified me that the bull wasn't in his pen yesterday morning about eight. I hurried to the location and saw that the padlock had been cut off. I immediately started a search of the rodeo grounds for Bulldog while I drove east, and Charlie, my second in charge, headed west, hoping to locate the bull before he did any damage. I also informed the police. Charlie called me at eight thirty when he came upon the bull and the family in their car. By the time I arrived, Charlie and Keith were coaxing the animal into his trailer."

"And the family is all right?" Cole asked in a matter-of-fact tone, as though they had never known each other.

"Yes, but not their car."

"What about the stolen petty cash?"

"Again, that happened at night in the last town we were in. The thief wasn't picked up on any cameras. There were no fingerprints that weren't supposed to be on the box. We had minimal security at the rodeo grounds in Silver Springs, but here, there were two guards on duty at night. They didn't hear or see anything."

"Can you add your own guards?"

"I've already done that. An extra two during the day and at night. Dad wasn't thrilled about the money we'll have to spend, but he's determined to catch this guy."

Cole scribbled something on his pad then looked up—trapping her with intense blue eyes that used to melt her. She shored up her defenses.

"How's your dad doing? I can't imagine him stopping long enough to recuperate." The hard, angular lines of Cole's face softened.

Her ex-husband and her father had gotten along great. Cole had become the son Red Richards never had. "He's fighting the doctor's orders tooth and nail. Mom has always been the only one who can get him to do anything. However, she has her hands full right now." Which was one reason Alexia was glad she was traveling a lot in the weeks to come.

Cole chuckled, the sound a surprise. "I imagine she does. He can be very stubborn."

"Yes, he can." Sometimes she'd wondered if Cole knew her dad better than anyone besides her mom. Alexia and Cole had dated her junior and senior years in high school. He'd been at their ranch all the time and often helped her dad. When she and Cole divorced, her father had blamed her. She hadn't discovered that until months after she returned to Montana to put her life back together. He never told her, but she'd overheard her parents talking about the divorce, and he made it clear that she hadn't work hard enough to keep their marriage together.

Cole rose. "I'd like to look around and talk with some of your employees."

She started to stand, but he waved his hand.

"Alone. Sometimes people will talk more freely when it isn't their boss."

"Okay. I certainly have work to do here."

As he started for the door, her phone rang.

Alexia rushed to answer Charlie's call.

"We have a problem with the show

tonight."

Cole glanced over his shoulder at her.

This was yesterday all over again. She raised her hand to stop his exit. "What's happened?" she asked Charlie.

TWO

Alexia clutched the phone even tighter as Cole moved back to stand behind the chair he'd sat in earlier.

"Marcie's too sick to ride tonight," Charlie said on the other end. "She missed rehearsing her act. I went to look for her and found her holed up in the bathroom, throwing up. When she came out, she was pale and exhausted. In fact, she hurried back into the room while telling me she must have picked up a stomach bug."

"She's never sick."

"Even if she feels better later, I doubt she'll eat much. She won't have enough energy to do her tricks. She's one of the acts the people love to watch." A long pause fell between them. "Do you think you could fill in for her?"

"I haven't performed in years, and I haven't practiced in a couple of months, not since I've been assisting Dad more." She peered toward Cole who took his seat again. "I'll have to rehearse and see if I can adjust to her equipment since mine's at the ranch."

"I could send someone to pick yours up."

"No. I don't want Dad to have another reason to worry, although I'm sure with his connections, he'll find out about this."

"I won't tell him," Charlie promised. "He's never going to recover if he doesn't let go of trying to control everything."

"I know."

Charlie's words rang in Alexia's mind. She'd learned the hard way her life could change instantly. Again, memories of her loss with her son's death taunted her and threatened to bring all that grief to the foreground when she'd finally managed to cope with what happened—or so she'd thought before Cole showed up. "I'll be out in the ring in an hour."

"I'll take Marcie to the motel then have Cutie Pie ready for you in the main arena."

When Alexia hung up the receiver, her gaze collided with Cole's hard blue eyes.

"When was the last time you performed in front of an audience?"

"Five and a half years ago before I became pregnant." She wouldn't look away first. She'd loved trick riding. So many things she'd enjoyed doing had been pushed to the background, and she'd turned her full attention to making it through a day one minute at a time. But now Cole's presence jeopardized her peace of mind.

Why is this all being stirred up again, Lord, when I've finally dealt with Daniel's death and put my life back together?

No, you haven't.

She bolted to her feet. "Like me, I'm sure you have work to do." She strode to the door and opened it, grasping the knob as though it would hold her upright.

Cole slowly rose. When he stopped in

front of her, she thrust her shoulders back and peered at him.

"I mourned our son, too," he said, a rasp in his voice.

"Halfway around the world." Before he treaded into territory she didn't want to go, she began pushing the door closed.

Cole's last look—forlorn and sad—tore at her composure. When the door clicked shut, she leaned against the wood, fighting to keep the tears inside.

Cole was *not* going to get to her.

Alexia retook her seat behind the desk and made the necessary calls before she finally headed for the arena. Charlie stood at one end next to a dark brown Quarter Horse. Having seen Marcie performing many times, Alexia had a sense of how the animal would act.

She approached Charlie and Cutie Pie. "How's Marcie doing?"

"I left her sleeping. I plan on checking with her after you practice."

"I'll come with you." She patted the horse then checked the special trick saddle. "Are you ready, Cutie Pie?" she asked before vaulting onto the mare's back.

Alexia rode around the arena at a trot then a canter before finally urging Cutie Pie into a gallop. She did a reverse neck layover then went into a side back bend. Sitting on the Quarter Horse, she relished the wind tugging at the strands of her hair as though it could whisk away her worries. All she concentrated on was the different tricks she would do. Nothing else occupied her mind. The sense of being free flowed through her.

* * *

After checking the pen where Bulldog had been kept, Cole inspected the others that housed their bulls. They appeared secured. He'd paid a visit to the police station to talk to the officer working the case. Detective Tom Samson didn't have any leads, and the security tape didn't reveal anything more than what Alexia had told him a few hours ago.

"So, the rumor's true. You're here to find out who caused Bulldog's release yesterday," a deep voice said behind Cole.

He turned and smiled at the two-time champion bull rider. "Keith, it's great seeing you again."

The tall, muscular man limped the few feet between them, taking Cole's hand and shaking it. "Charlie said you were here. Have you given up fighting for our country?"

"I figured after ten years, I needed to discover what it's like to be a civilian."

"And how is it?"

"I'm still adjusting." Especially with the reappearance of Alexia in his life. "Are you still riding bulls?"

"Nope. I had a bad accident six months ago. I thought I was ready to walk away, but as you see, I can't quite let go totally." Keith cocked a grin. "The rodeo life is in my blood."

"What are you doing?"

"I wanted to be a bullfighter, but I can't move fast enough." Keith slapped his right leg. "I'm a jack-of-all-trades. I'll be the announcer tonight. I understand that Alexia will be opening up the show since Marcie's sick. Alexia looked good rehearsing earlier."

When Alexia and Cole had dated as teenagers, he used to watch her perform all the time, but as they got serious, he'd wished she wouldn't. She'd never gotten hurt seriously, but she'd fallen off her horse several times. He hadn't minded putting himself in harm's way, but not Alexia. That was one reason he'd always played down his missions. If she'd known what he did in detail, that would have put a greater strain on their marriage. Being gone for weeks had done that enough. He hadn't wanted to add to it.

"Bulls are your specialty. What do you think happened with Bulldog? Any theories?"

Keith shrugged. "A disgruntled ex-employee. Red fired a guy right before he had his heart attack."

"Who?"

"Malcom Snyder. He came to work drunk one too many times."

"Have you seen him around?"

Keith shook his head. "But he doesn't live too far from Crescent City."

Cole passed his business card to him. "If you see him here, let me know."

"Will do. I'd better get changed into my fancy duds. People will start arriving soon to watch our show."

Across the way, Cole spied Alexia leaving the main building. She wore a hot pink sequined cowgirl shirt and pants. He cut across the grounds and fell into step next to her.

"How's Marcie doing?"

"Charlie and I took her to an after-hour clinic. I don't think there's anything else left to throw up. They were concerned about dehydration, so Charlie's with her while they give her IV fluids. Then he'll take her back to the motel. Her roommate will keep an eye on her."

"What did the doctor say about what made her sick? Is there a bug going around right now?"

"He thinks she ate something that didn't agree with her. She told the doctor where and what she had in case others come in sick like her."

Food poisoning? Could this be an

accident or something deliberate? It fit with the other two incidents. If he knew the why behind what was going on, he would be halfway to solving the crimes and returning to the quiet of the small ranch he'd recently purchased or to another case that wasn't so personal.

Alexia stopped. "Do you think whoever took the cash and let the bull out did something to Marcie to make her sick?"

"It's a possibility. When Marcie feels better, I'll talk to her. Food poisoning acts pretty fast, so if someone tampered with something she ate or drank, it was probably within a twenty-four-hour period."

"If that's the case, then I'm glad I can fill in for her. I don't want whoever's doing this to think he's getting to us."

"We'll talk after the show. I've been taking pictures all afternoon and will again tonight. I also set up several cameras in addition to those already in place. I made sure no one saw where I put them."

The tension in her shoulders and face eased. "Thanks. I know being here and working with me is awkward, but I do appreciate the help."

Before he realized what he was doing, he reached for her hand and held it. "I'll always be here to help you and your father."

She tugged away from him, spun around, and marched to Cutie Pie's pen.

Cole watched her open the gate and enter the paddock. The Quarter Horse walked to Alexia and nudged her playfully. He shouldn't have mentioned Red to Alexia. Their relationship had always been precarious as long as he could remember, but he had the impression from tidbits he'd picked up while talking with people this afternoon that it had grown worse since she'd returned to Montana three years ago.

And he knew what was at the center of the change: the death of their son. He still mourned the loss of Daniel every day. He'd let Alexia down when she'd needed him the most. Because he'd been behind enemy lines, he'd been cut off from his base and didn't even know about Daniel dying until a week afterward. Then it took him twenty-four hours to fly back to Georgia. By that time, Alexia had shut down, and he couldn't reach her. They talked when it was necessary. Otherwise, they were two strangers living together.

A lanky cowboy approached the paddock where Alexia was and leaned against the wooden slabs, staring at her. Who was he? The guy said something to her he couldn't hear. But when she answered the man, a look of irritation wrinkled her brow.

Cole took out his cell phone, zoomed in on the stranger, and took a picture. Since he was where only the workers should be, he might be part of the show. He'd ask Charlie about the cowboy.

Cole moved closer, intending to stay near as long as that guy hung around Alexia. When she took Cutie Pie's reins and led the mare out of her pen, the man hooked his thumbs in his jeans and sauntered away in the opposite direction.

Keith announced the show would begin in five minutes.

Cole made his way to a spot he'd scouted out earlier to position himself during the performance. He couldn't see everything going on, but it gave him a good vantage point for the events in the show as well as the chutes for the bull and bronco riders.

He took a few more photos then searched for Alexia. She appeared, mounted on Cutie Pie, stopped at the main entrance into the ring, and leaned over to pat the mare. Keith introduced her, and the gate opened. She galloped around, dismounting and springing back up onto the saddle facing backward. She circled the arena two times going through several tricks, including the difficult suicide drag where she leaned over backward with her hands brushing the ground.

When she slowed by the entrance, the cowboy from earlier jogged out with a banner for her. He held the reins while she positioned herself for the hippodrome. Other performers lined up behind Alexia along with a little boy on a horse. He must be the child in the car that Bulldog attacked. The cowboy laid the reins near the saddle then gave her the banner.

"Ladies and gentlemen, Alexia Richards is opening the show followed by the various entertainers who will thrill you with their skills."

Alexia kicked Cutie Pie into a canter then a lope, popping up into her stance holding the banner for the show. As the line of performers passed by, the crowd stood and applauded.

Cole couldn't take his eyes off Alexia. She made it seem so easy when he knew it wasn't.

Halfway around the arena, Alexia wobbled and suddenly went down forward and to the right, her left foot momentarily lodged in the hippodrome strap.

As others charged out of the gate, Cole hopped over the fence and rushed toward Alexia, who was now on the ground.

Cole's heart kept up with each pounding step.

THREE

Cole paced from one end of the ER waiting room to the other. He should be in there with Alexia, but he'd stayed behind to investigate what caused her fall from Cutie Pie and to talk with a police officer at the Founders' Day Celebration. Cole was determined to discover who tried to harm her. She could have died from that fall. At least, Charlie was inside with her. He'd come out and told Cole that it was a clean ankle break so no surgery would be required. Instead, she would be wearing a cast.

Anger swelled in his chest, making breathing difficult as he reenacted what happened in his mind—watching Alexia as she fell to the hard ground during her trick riding. The hippodrome strap on the right side gave way, causing her to tilt and lose her balance. She'd tried to squat and grab the mare's mane, but it happened so fast she tumbled to the ground when her left foot finally slipped free.

After he examined the strap, he'd called the detective he'd talked to earlier at the police station and reported the incident. No accident, but deliberate tampering. Because he didn't know who to trust, he'd taken the trick riding saddle and locked it in his truck so he could show it to the detective tomorrow morning.

He spied a coffee machine on a counter and headed toward it. It might be a long night. He planned to review the footage from the cameras he'd installed and the official one that Red always had made of his shows. He wasn't sure if the job was an inside one or if someone outside was trying to get to Alexia or her father's business. There weren't that many times the saddle would have been available for someone to tamper with it. Earlier in the day, Alexia had checked to make sure the equipment was in good condition. Had she inspected it again before her performance?

Cole started to pour another cup of the caffeine-laden brew when he spotted Charlie and Alexia. She used a knee walker to take the pressure off her left ankle. He set the coffeepot down then hurried to her. "I'd like to drive you to the motel."

Alexia looked at him for a long moment then turned her attention to Charlie. "Thanks for being with me. Would you make sure that Marcie is all right? I'd planned to stop by after the show to let her know how everything went. I'll have to do it tomorrow when I get used to this scooter you insisted I use for a while even though I have a walking cast." She gave the older man a brief smile.

"Sure."

Cole released a long breath. He had been prepared to insist Alexia ride with him so they could talk privately about what happened. "If Marcie hasn't already heard, she needs to know Cutie Pie's all right. I had the vet look over the mare before I came to the hospital."

"That's a relief." Alexia started forward, her jaw set in a hard line as she wrestled with the scooter.

When Cole and Alexia arrived at his Chevy truck, he came to her side. "Lean on me. I'll help you up into the cab." He clasped her upper arm.

She stiffened for a few seconds then relaxed to allow him to assist her into the pickup. "This cast is going to make it difficult to get in and out of my truck. At least I can drive since it's my left ankle."

"I think for the time being I should chauffeur you where you need to go." He shut the passenger door, rounded the hood, then climbed behind the wheel.

"I can manage by myself."

"Let's not argue over this. You might be in danger. The strap was tampered with. You were meant to fall."

"It wasn't even common knowledge I was going to fill in for Marcie until late this afternoon."

"You know how fast rumors can travel. I

have a suspicion that Marcie may have been fed something to make her sick. You're the only one who could fill in for her in such a short time."

Alexia didn't say anything else until they pulled into the parking lot of the motel nearest the rodeo grounds. "Where are you staying tonight?"

"Right here in my truck. The motel was full when I tried to get a room. Charlie offered me a bed, but I don't have a good feeling about what happened to you. If someone's angry with Red or the company, he might think getting to you would hurt both."

Alexia laughed, no humor in the sound. "Then they don't know about my relationship with my father."

"Your dad loves you. He's just not a demonstrative man."

"You haven't been around the past three years. If it hadn't been for Mom, I'm not sure I would have been working for him when I returned to Montana."

Cole twisted toward Alexia, the pain in her voice drawing him. He wanted to comfort her. He even leaned closer, but in the dim light from the motel, her stiff posture shouted, "Do not touch."

She bit into her lower lip and turned her head away for a long moment. Finally, she glanced toward him. "You're working for the Red Richards Rodeo Company. I can't have you camping out in your truck. I have two queen beds. You can use one. Then tomorrow we'll deal with finding you a place to sleep."

He opened his door. "Stay put. I'll help you down." She could be determined, and he didn't want her to do something to make her ankle worse.

As he assisted her from his cab, she leaned against him, and he caught a whiff of the scent she'd worn since she was a teenager. The vanilla fragrance brought back memories: holding and kissing her, making love to her. An ache deep in his gut spread. She'd always been independent, determined to do things on her own, and the one time she'd needed him he'd been thousands of miles away. Then and now, she shut herself off from him. He'd never forget the look she'd given him back then—bleak, hopeless, and angry. He'd needed to grieve for his son and had hoped they could do so together.

That never happened.

As soon as she could, she put some distance between them and rolled her knee scooter toward the motel room door, which she had opened by the time he grabbed his duffel bag from his truck.

The tension mounted as he entered behind her. She looked at the blinking light on the motel's phone and gripped the scooter handles so hard her knuckles whitened. "If I'd had my cell phone on me during the ride, my phone would have been ringing before I got to the hospital."

"You can return calls tomorrow. It's twelve thirty." Cole put his bag down by a chair.

"I wish I could. If it's Dad calling, he'll keep at it until I answer." She maneuvered her scooter between the beds, eased down on one, and listened to the messages.

When she hung up, she didn't have to tell him that it was her father. Resolve set into her expression. She would deal with him as she had for years—one careful step after another.

As Alexia reclined against the headboard, she raised her left leg onto the mattress, the strain after a long day evident on her face. When he realized that she was making the call to her father, he decided to give her some privacy. He stepped outside and left the door slightly ajar in case she needed him.

Who was he kidding? After years of trying to do everything right for her father, she'd rarely needed support, physically or emotionally, while they were married. Except after Daniel's death. But even if he'd been there, he didn't know if she would have accepted any comforting from him.

Leaning against the outside wall, he scanned the parking lot and the row of rooms at the motel. A door opened at the far end of the first floor. Charlie emerged, saw Cole, and headed his way.

"How's she doing?" Charlie asked, stopping in front of Cole.

"She's talking with her dad right now. How about Marcie? Is that her room?" Cole gestured in the direction Charlie had come.

"Yeah. She's finally looking better. I waited until she fell asleep before I left."

"Good. In light of what happened with Alexia, I'm going on the assumption someone gave her something that made her sick."

Charlie removed his cowboy hat and ran his fingers through his hair. "That's what I'm thinking, too. We're gonna have to check all the equipment frequently and right before using it." He glanced toward the door to Alexia's room. "Do you need to stay with me tonight?"

"No. I'm staying with Alexia."

Charlie's eyes widened.

"To protect her if someone is after her," Cole said. "That's all. Don't read anything else into it."

"That's a shame. You two were great together. I know Red would love to welcome you back into the family."

"Too much has happened between us."

"That doesn't mean you can't forgive

and move forward. Don't forget I watched you two fall in love."

"What does tomorrow entail?"

"Another show. A little different. It's for Mayor Bailey's birthday."

Cole whistled. "That's not a cheap party."

"I think Red gave him a deal. After all, they're friends from their days spent on the rodeo circuit. Then we travel to the last town where there'll be a rodeo. Some of our guys and gals will be participating, and others will be the entertainment."

"Nothing happened at the first two towns?"

Charlie plopped his hat back on his head. "Nope."

"Did you add any new workers between the second and third place?"

"Nope."

"Is there anyone working for Red who has a beef with him?"

Charlie scratched his beard. "A few, but usually those don't last."

"Who's been fired recently?"

"Only three in the last year: Buddy

Wills, Malcolm Snyder, and Don Chambers."

"Do you know where they are?"

"Actually, Don and Malcolm live near Crescent City. Buddy was on the rodeo circuit the last I heard. He'll be in the next town most likely." Charlie tried to suppress a yawn but couldn't. "I'd better head to bed. Tomorrow's gonna be a busy day." Charlie sauntered away.

Maybe Cole wasn't the right person for this job. Michael could find someone to take Cole's place. Yes, he knew a lot of the old timers who'd worked for Red for years, but what if one of them was behind the sabotage? Red wasn't an easy man to work for. He might pay his employees well, but he demanded a lot from them. His temper flared easily, but he didn't hold grudges.

"Cole, I'm finished."

Nothing in Alexia's tone indicated how well the conversation with her father had gone. But the second he stepped into the motel room, he could tell it had been stressful. "What did your dad say?"

"He was surprised you were here but

glad. He wants you to call him. I told him he'd have to wait until tomorrow morning. Much to my surprise, he didn't demand I find you and hand the phone to you."

"In the morning would be good. I want his take on who could be doing this. I talked with Charlie a few minutes ago. He told me Buddy Wills, Malcolm Snyder, and Don Chambers were fired this past year. I'm going to investigate them. What do you think? Any other suspects?" Cole sat on the queen bed across from Alexia's.

She stared at her lap for a long moment. "I agree they could be behind this, especially Don, who flicked a cigarette onto the ground in the barn when my dad fired him in front of several employees. Charlie's quick reflexes stopped a fire from starting. There's one more, but he still works for my father. Sammy Lincoln. The only reason he's still there is he's a distant cousin. I'm not sure why he's even working for the company. He's lazy and impulsive."

"Red has quite a few family members working for him."

"Yeah, that's why he started the

company in the first place." Alexia shifted her legs over the side of the bed, pulled the scooter close and stood, then headed for the bathroom.

Cole pulled out his cell phone and listed the names of the possible suspects. After Alexia returned, he checked the windows and door to make sure they were locked then took his turn in the restroom. When he came back into the main room, Alexia's eyes were closed, her features more relaxed. He turned off all the lights and reclined on his bed. His mind swirled with suspects and information surrounding the incidents. None of it made sense. To figure out who was after Alexia, he needed to come up with the reason behind the attacks.

Slowly sleep descended, and Cole surrendered to it...

The blast from the hidden bomb lifted Cole from the ground and flung him forward. The hard impact with the dirt road stunned him, momentarily robbing him of a decent breath. Opening his eyes, he tried getting up, but his world tilted and spun.

When he could finally focus on the person nearest him, pain contorted his buddy's mouth, but Cole couldn't hear his screams. He pushed to his knees, determined to stand. Again he couldn't as though he were caught up in the swirl of a tornado. Nauseated, he crawled toward his friend— to help. When he reached Nate, Cole managed to kneel next to him, his vision stabilizing. He fixed on a piece of shard piercing Nate's chest, blood flowing from the wound.

He locked gazes with Nate. "I'm here."

His friend's eyes grew round.

Suddenly Cole held his son, Daniel, against his chest. A sound drew Cole's glance to the side. An enemy, gun raised, ran toward him.

"No! No!"

His scream filled his ears as Cole bolted up in bed, sweat pouring off him.

FOUR

"No!" yanked Alexia from a groggy sleep. She sat up as another gut-wrenching "no" echoed through the air. The sound sent her heart beating at a rampaging rate.

She scooted to the edge of the mattress. The dim light leaking through the curtains allowed her to see Cole sitting straight up on his bed as through frozen in place.

"Cole? Are you all right?"

Silence.

"Cole, what's wrong?" Alexia used the nightstand to maneuver herself to his bed without using her left leg. Even with a walking cast, she wanted to keep pressure off that leg as much as possible.

When she reached out slowly and touched him, she felt his tremors, and her heart hurt for him. She ran her hand up and down his arm, but the quivering lingered. His continued silence worried her.

She leaned toward the lamp nearby, switched it on, and glanced at him. Anguish left deep lines in his face.

"Turn it off," Cole said in a raspy, rugged voice.

She did, but she couldn't forget his expression. Cole had always been strong, reserved, and quiet. In all the years they had known each other, she'd never seen him like this.

"What's wrong?" she asked again.

He flung himself toward the end of the bed and scrambled off it. The sound of him pulling air into his lungs filled the room.

Before she could respond to his sudden move, he headed toward the exit and opened it.

"Where are you going?"

"Nowhere." Then he slipped outside,

closing the door.

She couldn't sit there and wait for him to return. She shouldn't care about whatever he was dealing with, but they had once been best friends and lovers. They'd had a child together.

Again, she turned on the lamp, rolled the scooter closer, and stood. Then she maneuvered it to door and left to find Cole. At the very least she could be with him even if she didn't say anything. She wouldn't push this time.

She spied him across the parking lot, sitting on a bench with a view of her motel room. The warm spring air caressed her as she covered the distance between them. He didn't move, other than to tense when she eased down next to him. All she did was put her hand on his jean-clad thigh to let him know he wasn't alone.

His look and the sound of his voice had reminded her of when she'd tried to make sense of Daniel's death. She still couldn't.

Ten minutes passed before Cole laid his hand over hers. "Thanks."

"Did you have a nightmare?" After her

son died, she couldn't even sleep for days because all she saw was Daniel just out of arm's reach.

"Yes. I haven't had one in months."

"About the war?" She'd heard about veterans dealing with bad dreams because of what they went through, and Cole had spent many years on top-secret missions, losing his battle buddies.

He didn't answer.

She didn't have the right to push him to talk, and if it was about his combat experiences, he wouldn't tell her anyway. He'd always kept that part shut off from her.

She peered at the eastern sky beyond the motel building. Streaks of rose, purple, and yellow splashed across the sky, announcing a new day. "Remember when we used to get up early to watch the sun rise. I still do that when I can because it always calms me before the day begins."

"So do I." He rose, still holding her hand. When he tugged, she stood. "I don't know about you, but I'm starving. I didn't get dinner last night."

"Me neither." As though on cue, her stomach growled. "As you can tell." She chuckled.

While they slowly made their way back to the motel room, Alexia slanted a look in his direction. The strong lines of his profile reassured her he would catch the culprit behind the incidents. He always exuded confidence and self-assurance.

Except for the brief moment earlier when he'd first awakened.

* * *

The next day, Cole drove behind Alexia in the Red Richards Rodeo's convoy. They were only a few miles from Moose Creek, the locale of the last show before returning to the Flying Red Ranch after a two-week road trip. Last night's performance had gone smoothly. Was it because of the beefed-up security? He hoped so. Maybe then the one performance in Moose Creek might go off without an incident.

The night before, Alexia had been wound so tightly she hadn't stayed around long to celebrate the employees last night in Crescent City. Charlie had planned it to boost everyone's spirits after what had been going on lately.

Cole had stayed with Alexia again because a gut feeling kept telling him she was one of the targets of the unknown assailant. But the whole night he'd barely slept. He didn't want to have another nightmare. He'd thought he'd dealt with all that last year. Obviously not, but he knew why. Alexia. How could he tell her that in his dream as he tried to protect his friend from being shot by the enemy that he'd held Daniel in his arms, his son screaming and flailing his arms and legs?

He couldn't save Daniel—or his buddy, Nate. Cole survived, but they hadn't. He had to deal with that every day. A father was supposed to protect his child. The mounting deaths of people around him drove him from continuing his service to his country.

His tight grip on the steering wheel sent pain up his arms. He shook the memory from his mind and focused on where he was before he had an accident.

He pulled into a parking space next to Alexia's pickup, not even sure how he'd ended up here. Before he could help her down, she climbed from her truck and looked toward him. At least she must have gotten rest last night. Color had returned to her cheeks, and with a good show last night, a sparkle had returned to her brown eyes.

At the Flying Red Ranch, she would be safer at the main house than in a motel room. He needed to feel he could leave her and that she'd be all right so he could investigate who was behind the sabotage.

"That's the kind of trip I'll take every time—an uneventful one." Alexia stopped in front of his truck. "I have to go check in with the rodeo grounds' office. Then we should grab something to eat."

"Together?" At breakfast, she'd sat with a group of women who worked for RRR Company, and the last day in Crescent City, he'd been working with the police about the two incidents and making sure security was tight for the final performance while Charlie stuck with her. He was the only one Cole trusted to be with Alexia when Cole wasn't there to protect her.

"I figure we need to talk about what's been going on before we head back to the ranch tomorrow. Yesterday, we were busy and never talked about what's happening and who might be behind the trouble. It's my job to be on top of this."

Every call she'd had with her father had reinforced that in Alexia. She'd never said anything after talking with Red, but she'd looked drained, emotionally and physically. Her father hadn't always been so hard on her. What had changed?

"Lunch sounds fine. I'm going to walk around to figure out where I want to put my cameras." And there were a few employees he hadn't gotten to know. Two somehow had avoided him, and he'd decided to track them down. One had been a friend of Don Chambers and had met with Chambers last night after the show.

"Good. Let's meet here in half an hour." She gave him a small grin then made her way toward the entrance of the building, limping. She'd given up the scooter and relied on her walking cast.

He hurried ahead of her and opened the door for her.

Her smile grew to encompass her whole face. "It still feels strange with this walking cast but easier than using crutches or a scooter."

He watched her until she disappeared into an office down the hall at the end. With a sigh, he turned away and set out to find Paul Raymond, Chambers' friend. Cole found him unloading the horses. He stood back and observed him for a few minutes before approaching.

"Do you need any help?" Cole asked when Raymond released a mare into a paddock. "I have some time to kill before going to lunch with Alexia."

"Sure."

"By the way, I'm Cole Knight."

"I'm Paul Raymond." He shook Cole's hand. "I heard you're here because of the accidents."

"Do you think they're only accidents?"

Raymond shrugged.

Cole strode next to the wrangler. "I noticed you're a friend of Don Chambers. I was surprised he would come to a Red Richards' Rodeo Production."

"Why? It's a free country, and he's a friend of the mayor."

"From what I heard, Chambers wasn't too happy with Red when he fired him." Cole took the reins of the horse Raymond gave him then started back toward the pens.

"Don was fine with it. He was gonna quit anyway. He wanted to move back to Crescent City, and the boss can be difficult to work for."

"Is that what you think or Chambers?"

"Chambers. Not me." The wrangler took the reins of both animals and released them inside the paddock then closed and latched the gate.

"Have you seen anyone suspicious around lately?"

"A homeless guy at dawn the day Bulldog ran rampant through the town."

"Was he near the paddock where the bull was kept?"

"Not when I saw him, but he'd come from that area. I chased him away. He had no business being at the rodeo grounds."

"Why do you think the person was homeless?"

"His clothes were dirty with holes in them. He had short—no medium length, scraggly hair. Also, he wore a beard as unkempt as his hair."

"Why didn't you tell Alexia or Charlie about the guy?"

The wrangler shrugged. "Never had the opportunity."

"Thanks, I'll let the police in Crescent City know about the man." Cole wanted to see Raymond's reaction to the mention of the police and also to let him know he would be checking the information the wrangler gave him.

Raymond blinked several times, and in the process of turning away from Cole, he said, "He could've just been passing through. He carried a dirty knapsack."

"Did you see him any other time?"

The cowboy shook his head. "I've gotta go. I need something to eat before we rehearse the stagecoach robbery for tonight."

After his conversation with Paul Raymond, Cole walked around the rodeo grounds, noting the places where he'd put his cameras after he had lunch with Alexia. Maybe he would discover the reason behind the change in Red since he'd last seen him—at Daniel's funeral. The memory trapped emotions in his throat.

* * *

When Alexia left the office, she spied Cole talking to a man at the end of the hall near the exit. Maybe she would learn what had upset him so much the other night when he woke up from his nightmare. She still could hear the anguish in the two words he shouted. When they sat together on the bench later that night, he hadn't said much. They had always shared their thoughts before their son died. But Daniel's death had changed everything. She wasn't the same person and neither was Cole. They were like strangers.

If they were going to work together, she needed to put the past behind her. The tension of what occurred three years ago twisted her stomach into knots. She'd needed him, and he'd let her down. *How do I get past that?* She knew what God wanted her to do. To forgive him. Perhaps she could, but she didn't think she could ever forgive herself for what happened to Daniel. And if Cole knew it was her that let their son die, he'd never forgive her either.

She limped down the hallway, catching Cole's attention out of the corner of his eye. He said something to the man he was talking to then walked toward Alexia. A smile slowly transformed his tanned face. His blue eyes gleamed. His glance tingled down her body, and goose bumps rose on her arms.

"I'm starving," she said, trying to concentrate on something else beside her reaction to him. "A muffin and coffee wasn't enough for breakfast. The manager of the rodeo grounds told me the diner across the street has some of the best food in the area."

"And close, too. Sounds good." Cole held the door open for her. "You're getting around well."

"I have to. After lunch, I'm going to see the sheriff. I'm hiring a few off-duty deputies for extra security tonight. Actually, the sheriff is a friend of Dad's. The sheriff's coming to the rodeo, but he wanted me to fill him in on what's been occurring in the other towns."

"I think Red is friends with half of Montana."

"Probably." Her father could be demanding and tough as an employer, but he was also a loyal friend to many and would go the extra mile for them if needed. "I always wished I was one of those he called a friend."

Pausing to cross the street, Cole grasped her hand. "What happened with you two? I know he can be demanding, but you two had a good relationship."

In the midst of the warm air, a chill engulfed her. "He thinks he knows what's best for me."

"He's always felt that way, but you two

got along."

"If we're going to eat lunch, I don't want to discuss my dad. I've lost enough sleep lately because of him. His heart attack came out of the blue. He almost didn't make it. We have our issues, but I still care about him in spite of our problems." If only her father felt that way toward her. She used to think he did, but after overhearing him tell her mother that she should have found a way to get to Daniel before she got out of the burning house, she'd learned differently. His words had hurt beyond repair.

"I'm sorry you two are going through a tough patch." Cole entered the crowded café behind Alexia. After they sat at a table, he added, "Unless we find the person responsible for what's going on, Red wants me to come back to the ranch and work on the case from there."

"When did he tell you that?"

"My last phone conversation with him. I told him I didn't think what was happening would necessarily stop when everyone returned to the ranch."

"You think this will follow us there?"

He nodded. "Especially if it's a worker or even a disgruntled ex-employee."

After the waitress approached and took their orders, Alexia took a long sip of her water. "Who do you suspect after these few days hanging out with us?"

"I've talked with everyone except Becca Norman. I'm beginning to feel she's avoiding me."

"Becca? She's been with us for a few years. Her roping skills are superior. The audiences love her. Why do you think she's avoiding you?"

"I've entered a room where she was a couple of times, and she got up and left. Once she looked right at me before ducking out."

"I'll make sure Becca comes to see you. I have to talk to her later. I'm thinking of using her in my place with the stagecoach robbery. I know I'm only a passenger, but I'll have to get out of the coach when the robbers stop it. That will be awkward with my walking cast although my long dress will cover my legs."

"But you haven't decided yet?"

She shook her head. "I'm usually part of it. When it's over, I join Keith to announce the beginning of the show. I could still do that, but a passenger dealing with a cast would seem strange to the audience."

"Either way, I'll talk with her before or after the heist tonight."

She chuckled, glancing around. "Shh. Don't say that too loud. We might be reported to the sheriff."

Cole winked at her. "Good thing you have an in with him."

For a few seconds, his teasing tone reminded her of their carefree days as a couple before his job took him away more and more and he stopped sharing what was going on with her. "Who else stands out as a potential person behind what's happening?"

"Nothing concrete. Don Chambers attended the mayor's birthday party last night. I saw him and Paul Raymond meeting after the show. Chambers gave Raymond something. I couldn't tell what.

When I finally talked with Raymond today, he played down Chambers being fired and told me about a homeless guy hanging around in Crescent City. When I reviewed the tapes, I never saw anyone fitting that description."

"Trying to divert your attention?"

"Possibly. Besides meeting with the sheriff, what else are you doing today?"

"I'll be with Charlie going over the final details. Marcie's going to ride today. When I saw her this morning, I told her I would understand if she didn't perform. That's when she told me she was a lot better. She's going to perform at the end but not do the hippodrome until she can get the strap repaired."

"Before she rides, I'd feel better if I look over her saddle. Is that okay?"

"Sure, but she already assured me she would." Alexia waited until the waitress put her chef salad in front of her then left before she continued. "She feels bad about what happened to me. She was getting ready to ride until she had another bout of nausea and realized she wouldn't be doing the show any favors."

"You said she's been with the show for a while."

"Yeah, she came about four years ago. My dad saw her talent and worked with her on her trick riding. She's garnering quite a reputation."

"Does that bother you?"

"No. Why would it?"

"That was you before you left with me for Georgia. Until the strap broke, you were riding like you did years ago."

"I'm the one who suggested Marcie take my place." Had she ever felt jealous when she watched her dad and Marcie working in the ring at the ranch? If she was truthful with herself, she had been envious for a—minute. She really enjoyed managing the company. That had been clear when she'd been given the opportunity to run the five-town road trip.

While they ate their lunch, Alexia kept their conversation on the investigation. "How about the employees Dad fired? Anything pointing to one of them."

"Other than Don Chambers' meeting

with Raymond at the mayor's birthday party, the others haven't been spotted in the vicinity of the rodeo. Your father may be a tough boss, but he hadn't fired many workers in the last four years."

"Have you thought about another company like the RRR?"

"Like who?"

"There's a ranch near the Flying Red that started doing what we do. Parker Franklin. He bid on this rodeo here, but Dad undercut him. Also the one in Crescent City."

"You should have told me this sooner."

"I forgot about it until just now. Parker was furious and had a shouting match in town with Dad right after the approval of our bid for the show."

"I'll take a look at him." Cole finished the last bite of his hamburger and motioned to the waitress to come to the table. When she approached, he said, "Check please for both meals."

"I'll bring it right away."

As the young woman left, Alexia leaned toward him. "I'm paying. This was business."

For a moment, silence hung between them. He fixed his gaze on her. She didn't back down. Their relationship had to remain strictly a professional one, and her paying was a good reminder to him.

When the waitress came back and handed him the check, he passed it to Alexia. "The next one, for business or pleasure, is on me."

The word pleasure kicked up her pulse rate a notch. Her mind flooded with memories of their times together, laughing and loving. And for a few heartbeats, she missed those days, but when she spotted Marcie entering the diner with several others from RRR, reality returned. She had to do everything she could to keep her employees safe.

She placed the money for the lunches on the bill then rose. "I need to get back to work. I don't have much time until I meet with Sheriff Woods."

When they stepped outside in the late spring day, Cole walked next to her. "And I need to finish my reconnaissance of the rodeo grounds and find places for my cameras that aren't already covered by the ones in place."

Reconnaissance. She knew when they married six years ago that Cole was a soldier. She'd prepared herself for the months he would be gone overseas where she couldn't go. That was when she turned her full attention to learning how to manage RRR. She had to stay busy. Then he was stationed in Georgia, and she moved to live on base with him. Although the absences were weeks instead of months, when Cole would come back home, each time a part of him became more locked away from her. He couldn't talk about his job, and she'd wanted to know every detail of his life. Even with a job on base, she'd needed more to make her life fulfilled.

Then she became pregnant, and she found a purpose. She wanted to be a mother to more than one child. Daniel became her focus. When Cole was at the base, the three of them did everything together. And she was okay with the situation. She found contentment in her baby and the time she had with her husband.

"This is where we part ways." Cole's deep voice cut into her thoughts. "If you need me, call my cell phone. See you later."

As she watched him stroll away, she determinedly focused on the present—not the past. God was right. Live in the moment. Don't worry about the unknown future or agonize over what had already happened. If she repeated it enough, maybe she would believe it.

* * *

Cole sat on the chute fence, giving him a good vantage point for the start of the program and of Alexia watching the show. The nearby gates at one end of the ring opened wide, and the stagecoach, drawn by four mares, shot out of the opening. When it reached the mid-field point, the robbers with handkerchiefs covering most of their faces, charged out after the coach, firing their guns. The loud sounds reverberated through the rodeo grounds.

The audience encouraged the driver—Charlie—with shouts to keep going. The cowboy sitting next to Charlie slumped over as though he'd been shot. As the thieves gained on the coach, one of the passengers fired his weapon out the window. The driver slowed down.

The leader of the gang aimed his gun at the people inside. "Stop or I'll shoot each one of you."

Charlie, as rehearsed earlier that afternoon, pulled back on the reins and stopped the horses.

The crowd fell silent, as though everyone held their breath and waited to see what would happen next.

In the quiet, a scream coming from inside the stagecoach pierced the air, its sound chilling. Cole jumped down from the fence, turned to one of the security guards and said, "Keep Alexia here." Then he raced into the ring.

FIVE

The audience was on its feet clapping and shouting. The attendees must have thought the scream was part of the show. Cole increased his speed.

His boots pounded the ground, vying with the thudding of his heartbeat. He reached the stagecoach on the left side at the same time the robbers dismounted and hurried toward the carriage on the right.

As Cole yanked open the door, chaos greeted him. One of the wranglers inside the stagecoach held Becca in his arms, blood flowing from her shoulder, while the other two passengers scrambled out of the coach. The first robber grabbed the handle and pulled the opposite door open.

"What happened?" Cole asked the cowboy still inside.

"I was returning fire and suddenly Becca slumped against me. Kendra screamed when she saw the blood. We use blanks. This shouldn't have..." The young man's face paled, and he tossed his gun down as though the bullet had come from his weapon.

The audience quieted, a siren in the distance the only sound. Two police officers converged on the coach while the people in the stands began fleeing, finally realizing something was wrong.

Cole helped the wrangler lay Becca on the seat then glanced toward the entrance to the rodeo ring. The doctor on call, holding a black bag, ran toward them. "I've got this," Cole said to the cowboy. "Leave your gun and go."

When the doctor arrived, Cole moved to make room for him. "She was shot in the right shoulder."

The older man climbed inside and examined Becca while one of the police officers poked his head in the window. Cole repeated what he'd told the doctor.

"We're clearing the rodeo arena. Let's get this stagecoach out of the ring. Move it slowly to the double gates."

"Okay." Cole exited the door, noticing Charlie who'd driven the coach was leaving with the other officer and the participants in the robbery. Cole climbed up, took the reins, and headed for the ring's exit. He surveyed the area. Where had the shot come from? One of the robbers or someone else? It wasn't anyone up close to Becca.

As the stagecoach neared the exit, Cole caught sight of Alexia with a deputy next to her. Their gazes connected across the small expanse. From her creased forehead, pinched mouth, and rigid stance, he didn't have to read her mind to know what she was thinking. She hated being confined by the officer. She wanted to be where she could make sure everyone was escaping safely. But mostly she was worried about Becca.

One thing dominated his thoughts: Becca had replaced Alexia as a passenger. Her name wasn't changed in the program because Alexia didn't make the decision until half an hour before the show. She'd finally realized she couldn't do everything when she couldn't move around as fast as she usually did.

Was the shot random or had someone thought the woman in the black veiled hat was Alexia, not Becca?

After they passed through the open gates, Cole slowed the coach and brought it to a stop near where the EMTs had parked the ambulance.

After Cole jumped to the ground, he made sure Becca was being taken care of and protected by the police officer in the stagecoach. Cole searched for Alexia. He didn't intend to leave her side.

When he found her, she was talking to Keith, who left when Cole joined them. "You need to get inside somewhere."

"I can't leave. I'm in charge."

Cole inched closer and leaned in toward her ear, whispering, "You won't be in charge if you're shot. That bullet might have been meant for you."

The color drained from her face. "I know Becca was a last-minute change, but it wasn't a secret I traded places."

"Not with the employees, but your

name was still in the program as a passenger."

"Then you think we have somebody following us from town to town?"

"Possibly. I'm going to let Charlie know we'll be in the rodeo grounds' office."

"Marcie needs a guard, too, because of what happened in Crescent City."

"I'll let Charlie know once you're in a safer place."

As Cole escorted Alexia to the office, he scanned the now deserted ring. There wouldn't be a program or a rodeo show tonight. The last two incidents made what was going on public. This would hurt Red's company. He wouldn't be surprised if venues cancelled their contracts with RRR. He had to find the person behind all this before someone was murdered or the company was driven out of business.

* * *

Alexia's prowling the manager's office at the rodeo grounds reminded her of the time she saw a tiger at a zoo doing the same thing. At the moment, she felt like roaring her frustration, but that would only alarm the deputy sheriff outside the door.

Earlier, she'd called her dad to let him know what happened, but he hadn't answered. She had to leave a message. She wasn't looking forward to that conversation. Then she got hold of her mother, so she'd know what was going on and could calm her father. One of his problems was high blood pressure, and this latest incident would send it skyrocketing.

When her cell phone rang, the sound startled her. She'd been expecting a call, but since Cole came back into her life, it didn't take much to scare her. His presence reinforced the fact that someone had a grudge, and that person didn't care who got in the way of his revenge.

After the fourth ring, she answered the phone. "You got my message, Dad?"

"No. I haven't listened to my voicemail. Sheriff Woods called me fifteen minutes ago and filled me in on what's going on. Then I called Cole after talking to Robert. He told me Becca's stable at the hospital, and that she took your place because of your cast. He thinks someone has targeted you or wants to get to me through you. As soon as Robert gives you the okay to leave, I want you all on the road. Come home." His voice caught at the end. She imagined he saw his dream for RRR being destroyed.

"It could be two or three days. The manager said we could stay here at the rodeo grounds until we're given the okay to pack up by the sheriff."

"Robert hopes only a day. He knows where our employees will be if he needs anyone."

"Are you all right?"

"Okay, in spite of all that's been occurring. I'm more concerned about you."

For a few seconds, what he said didn't really register until her father asked about how she was doing. He rarely did, and she wasn't prepared to answer.

"Alex? Are you still there?"

"Yes. I'm fine. I'm getting use to the walking cast. I…" She couldn't put into words what was really going on in her head. Sharing her feelings with her father hadn't been part of their relationship.

"Let Cole do the investigating. We'll talk more when you return to the Flying Red.

Bye."

He disconnected before she could recover enough to tell him good-bye. He actually sounded concerned—for her. He didn't even ask what she was doing to stop the sabotage. She couldn't even refer to it as that anymore. With the last two incidents where Becca and she had been hurt—could have died—the assailant had taken it to a different level. If not stopped soon, someone could die.

If her father thought she would sit back and do nothing to get this person, he would soon discover he was wrong. But then the man on the phone with her hadn't sounded like her dad. He'd almost sounded defeated. Her father was a fighter, and so was she. At the least, she would continue to work with Cole on the case before a person around her was killed.

A knock sounded on the office door. Then it opened, alerting her to Cole's return. Sheriff Woods followed behind him.

"I just talked to my dad. He said you called him."

The sheriff pushed his cowboy hat up and back. "Red and I go way back. I wanted to let him know I think, like Cole, that the assailant is escalating his attacks. An inch more and Becca Norman would have died."

"And we don't know for sure if the guy knew it was Becca, or if he thought it was you." Cole reclined against the desk in the middle of the room.

Alexia turned her attention to the sheriff. "Do you feel I'm the target, too?"

"We have to consider that. Two of the incidents involved you in some way. I'd rather be cautious than regret not doing something before it's too late. I'm assigning a deputy to stay with you when Cole can't be with you."

She put her hands on her waist. "Did anyone bother to ask me?"

"It's for one day." Cole straightened. "Your father would never forgive me if anything happened to you."

Despite the sheriff still in the office with them, Alexia thrust her shoulders back and faced her ex-husband. "I'll go with you. I want to help solve this, especially if my activities are going to be curtailed."

"Mostly, I'll be looking at videos of the

event. Maybe someone I saw on the tapes in Crescent City will be here, too."

"With my staff limited, that works for me. You two can view the tapes at the station and free up my deputy during that time." Sheriff Woods pulled his brim down. "We think the shot came from a distance, maybe the stands, but not from a performer in the skit. As soon as the bullet is removed from the victim's shoulder, we'll have evidence to tie someone to the shooting—if we find the gun."

"Wouldn't someone have noticed a shooter?" Alexia asked, not liking either implication of who might have shot Becca.

"There are a few places they could have hidden, one in particular that we checked," Cole answered. "There were a couple of cigarette butts on the ground nearby. The sheriff's going to try and get DNA off them. Rebecca's wound fits the angle of the shot from that area. The sound would have been covered up by the shootout taking place."

"We're still calculating the angle and projection by recreating the skit to determine a more exact location." Sheriff Woods took two steps back and turned partway, grasping the door handle. "Be careful, Alexia. I don't want to have to call Red to tell him something happened to you."

After the sheriff left, a silence fell between them until Cole said, "This is temporary. We should be back at the ranch the day after tomorrow. Your dad has a lot of loyal employees to help keep it safe."

"Unless it's one of the workers with us now."

"True, but as I'm reviewing tapes of your fall and Becca's shooting, I can rule out some of them. Like Charlie."

"You thought Charlie could have done this?"

"No, but it's nice to have proof it wasn't him. He was driving the stagecoach."

"Well, in that case, Keith was sitting next to Charlie and was pretending he'd been shot. So that's another one."

"And the other three passengers since the gun used wasn't fired at close range."

"It'll be nice not to suspect everyone I see and work with, but what if there's more than one person after us?"

Cole frowned.

"You've already considered that?"

He nodded.

"I want to know everything you do and who you suspect. I don't want you to shield me from the truth, or I'll make sure your job is more difficult."

"I will because I need your insight not because of your threats. I know you want the assailant found as fast as possible. So do I." Cole headed for the door. "Let's eat then take a drive to Great Falls to check on Becca. If she's awake, I'd like to ask her a few questions. If not, we can return tomorrow."

When Alexia stepped outside with Cole, she paused and scanned the area. She began to look for places where a sniper could have hidden. "What if the gunman wasn't in the crowd but holed up somewhere that he could shoot from a distance outside the arena? Like a sniper?"

Cole stiffened and turned his head away. "I've considered that, and the sheriff is checking on a couple of places."

"You did? Why didn't you say anything to me?"

"C'mon. Let's get into my truck. You

don't need to paint a target on your back."

Shivers flashed up her spine. *He really thinks I'm the one the assailant's after.*

Cole moved to his pickup and opened the passenger door.

As she hoisted herself up into the cab, she peered at his closed expression. "You haven't answered my question. What's going on?"

What little emotions on his face disappeared as he climbed behind the steering wheel. She'd never seen him like this. In all those times when he'd returned from a mission, even when he refused to tell her what had happened, he'd never seemed this far removed from her—so stoic.

SIX

The emotion-frothed silence in the cab of Cole's truck churned his gut. He'd never wanted to have this conversation with Alexia. She didn't need to be brought into his traumatic years as a soldier. He was dealing with it slowly with the Lord's help.

He started the engine and backed out of the parking space. "How about Moose Creek Steakhouse for dinner?"

For long moments, Alexia didn't respond. She stared out the passenger window, her arms folded over her chest.

When they'd dated and first married, there had been no secrets between them. Then he'd become a member of a Delta Force team, and a good part of his life became classified and covert. He'd lost the ability to share himself. That was the one reason he didn't fight Alexia on the divorce. He hadn't been in a good place even before Daniel died. Then their son's death sent him into a spiral that he'd thought would never end.

"Nothing fancy," Alexia finally said. "Fast food is fine with me. Then we can head to Great Falls right away. I need to personally make sure Becca will be all right."

"Don't blame yourself. It's not your fault."

"Who said I do?"

"Me. I've known you for years. Your tone of voice tells me."

"And I've known you for a long time, too, but you aren't the same person I married. That man wouldn't have evaded my question. Why didn't you tell me you thought it could be a sniper?"

That one word, *sniper*, rang through his mind. No comeback formed in his thoughts.

Instead, he turned into a fast food restaurant's drive-thru and asked, "What do you want to order?"

"A hamburger and fries with iced tea."

Her gaze cut through him, slicing his heart into two pieces. He should never have taken this assignment. He wasn't ready for the conversation she wanted from him.

He placed their orders then pulled around to the window and paid for the food. For the forty-five-minute drive to Great Falls, they ate their dinner but said nothing. Scenes from his last mission ran through Cole's mind. One member of his team after another being picked off by a shooter. Four soldiers died before he could take out the enemy's sniper in a cat-and-mouse "game" he wanted nothing to do with anymore.

* * *

After hours of watching yesterday's video tapes of the rodeo grounds from different angles, Alexia stifled a yawn yet again. She'd gotten little sleep last night. As she'd lain in bed, she'd relived each moment, and now she did so again at the sheriff's station.

She stood and stretched. "I guess it wasn't a total waste of time. We have a list of people we've eliminated as the shooter."

"And we still need to go through the footage from Crescent City." Cole closed the laptop. "Let's get out of here. We need to drive back to Great Falls. We can view the other tapes tonight at the motel. I'll arrange it with Sheriff Woods."

"I think that's a good idea. Becca was asleep when we were there last night. I'll feel better when I can talk to her."

"Me, too. She may know something that's important and not even realize it. According to Kendra, who was sitting across from her, she'd been staring out the window in the direction of the shooter."

"I didn't know that. When did you talk to Kendra?"

"I didn't. Sheriff Woods told me. He's working his way through all of your staff before we leave town tomorrow." Cole rose, arched his back, then twisted from side to side. "Ah, this feels so much better. It's good to get up. Even though we'll be sitting in the truck, our view will be a hundred times better than these four walls."

On the way out of the sheriff's office, Cole stopped to talk with him and let him know what they found in the footage—nothing as far as who could have pulled the trigger—and that they were driving to Great Falls to see Becca.

"How about the Rocky Mountain juniper near the arena? Did any of the cameras capture it on tape?" Sheriff Woods asked.

"Two but only the lower part of the tree."

"Thanks for checking. We might get more videos from the people attending the rodeo that will give us a better view of the whole tree."

Alexia paused before getting into his truck and faced Cole. "What's this about a juniper tree?"

"Yesterday when the sheriff and I looked at places that had good vantage points to fire a rifle at the stagecoach, that was the best one I found. It's a couple of hundred yards outside the arena."

"Oh. Why didn't you tell me to look for those?"

"I wanted you to focus on the people

who worked for you. The more of them we can rule out the better you'll feel when we go back to the ranch."

"I can do two things at once."

He chuckled. "I know you can. Here let me help you up into the truck."

"I've got this."

Alexia settled into her seat.

Cole rounded the hood, his attention focused on his surroundings. What was he keeping from her? Was this tied to their conversation yesterday, or did he know something about the case he didn't want her to know? She couldn't take the secrets. She'd understood why he had to keep them when they were married as far as his job went, but after a time, she'd realized the secrets had invaded their marriage. They'd stopped sharing like they used to.

As Cole drove in the direction of Great Falls, Alexia broke the silence. "What are you not telling me about the case? And don't tell me you aren't keeping something from me. I deserve honesty from you."

"I'm not being dishonest with you."

His grip on the steering wheel tightened until she wondered if he would snap it in two. "I have a feeling you aren't telling me everything concerning the case. You're acting like you did when you were going on a mission. Did you find a clue at the juniper?"

"No."

"But you think the shooter scaled the tree, made his shot from it, then climbed down without anyone seeing him?"

"Yes, because it's outside the rodeo grounds. Everyone was focused on the show, not the tree, so the shooter could have escaped without being seen. But I'd hoped someone with a phone had recorded him accidentally going up or down the juniper."

"That person had to be a good shot. Is the saboteur a sniper?"

"As you said, he's a good shot. Not necessarily a sniper. A good gunman can shoot over a mile away. The city water tank would have been a better perch."

"Did you work with a sniper in the military?"

The hard angles of his face with a nerve twitching in his jaw indicated she'd hit a bull's eye concerning what was bothering

Cole. The urge to ask more questions inundated her, but she wouldn't. If he wouldn't willingly tell her, then she needed to drop it. They weren't married anymore. After the case was solved, he'd return to his home, and they wouldn't have to see each other again.

She twisted her head around to stare out the side window. Disappointment weaved its way through her. She and Cole had known each other since they had been young teenagers. She hated admitting those years might not have meant as much to him as her. Tears filled her eyes, and she closed them. A wet track rolled down her cheek.

Minutes dragged out until soon the outskirts of Great Falls came into view. *Lord, please help us solve this case as soon as possible. I don't want to be around Cole. All I can think about with him around is our past. We had so many good times, but some weren't so great. Help me, Lord. How can I move on with him so near?*

Cole slowed down and parked off the highway.

"Why are we stopping?" Alexia asked,

turning her attention to him.

His expression of pain and exhaustion, as though he'd fought an inner battle and lost, bombarded the indifferent composure she was struggling to maintain.

He looked forward, out the windshield. "I know how snipers think because I was one the last couple of years of my service to my country. It's the reason I left the army. I have the ability but not the emotional stamina for that job. After Daniel's death, I was dead inside, and when my commander pushed me to be a sniper, I didn't fight him."

She knew what it felt like to be dead on the inside—still felt that way at times. Daniel had been her whole life for a year, and then he was suddenly snatched away and without Cole there. They'd needed each other, but instead of coming closer, they drew further apart.

His gaze swept to hers and bore into her as if he didn't even see her. "But over the next two years, I discovered I didn't have what I needed to do the job and walk away unharmed emotionally. I left the service this time last year, but I didn't

93

come home until six months ago because I was in a bad place. I went to counseling, and slowly the nightmares I used to have every night disappeared—until the other night. For the first time, Daniel was in the dream. I was holding him and an enemy was running toward us with his gun aimed at us."

The anguish in his words left her breathless, hurting inside for a man she'd loved once—possibly never stopped loving. She reached across the console and laid her hand on his arm. "I'm so sorry, Cole. We should have been there for each other. I was in a bad place, too."

He swallowed hard. "My counselor suggested I come see you when I returned to Montana. But I could never bring myself to do it. I didn't know what to say. I'm sorry I wasn't there for you."

"I wasn't for you either. All I could think about was that our son was gone and how I was going to live each day without him. I pushed you away because I didn't want another human being to get close to me. I couldn't go through losing someone again." As her confession tumbled from her, part of her was surprised by what she'd said, but then the meaning of the words sank in.

Through her blurry vision, she saw Cole twist toward her, taking her hand in his. "When this is over, we need to talk more and help each other to heal."

"I agree. We've known one another for over fifteen years. I think we definitely need to have a heart to heart. No more secrets between us."

He stared at her for a long moment then nodded. "Later. My top priority right now is keeping you safe. Let's go visit Becca and see if she can tell us anything useful."

"Sounds good. She's well-liked by the other employees."

"And so are you. That's why I'm beginning to feel it isn't a current worker." Cole started the engine and pulled out onto the highway.

As they continued their trip to Great Falls, Alexia wondered if the Lord was using what was happening to bring them together to finally resolve their past hurts.

* * *

Later that afternoon, Cole drove out of Great Falls, passing the place where he'd told Alexia about his days as a sniper and how Daniel's death had affected him, too. As a soldier, he'd done what he had to do, but those duties had taken a toll on him that he never thought about until he was in the middle of all that death and had to cope to survive.

"I was hoping Becca knew something that could help us."

Alexia's statement pulled Cole from his thoughts. "Yeah, I did, too, but it was a long shot that she'd seen anything beforehand."

"At least she should be released tomorrow. I'm going to have Charlie come over and pick her up while we're heading back to the Flying Red. I thought about us doing it, but if something happens to our convoy on the drive, I'll need to be there."

"And so do I." His confession to Alexia had lifted his spirits. He'd tried to ignore how troubled he'd been, and from the past, he knew that never worked for long. For years, he'd lived a secret life that he couldn't talk about other than with his team, which meant Alexia was excluded from a large part of his life. Coupled with many separations, not a good basis for a marriage.

"Where do we stand on the investigation? I know you talked with the police in Crescent City while we were in Great Falls. Anything from them?"

"Several others saw a homeless guy hanging around the rodeo grounds like Raymond had told me about. The detective managed to get a composite drawn. Here, take a look at what he sent me." Cole indicated his cell phone in a cup holder on his console. When Alexia picked it up, Cole put his thumb against the screen. "It should pop right up."

"That looks like a dirty version of Malcom Snyder. Did Detective Samson bring him in?"

"No, he can't find the guy."

"Which means he could have been involved with what happened in Moose Creek. You should talk to Charlie about him. I think he's a good shot, or at least, he bragged he was. Charlie might know because they went hunting together a couple of times while he worked at the Flying Red."

"If the homeless guy isn't in Crescent City, where is he? I'm going to show Sheriff Woods this composite picture. If he's in Moose Creek, then I think he goes to the top of the suspect list."

"I'm going to send this to myself as well as Dad and Charlie so I can get their thoughts on whether this could be Malcolm or not." Alexia bent forward, reaching for her purse on the floor.

Crack!

A bullet pierced the passenger window.

SEVEN

"**S**tay down! Someone's shooting at us," Cole yelled as he accelerated to get out of the shooter's range.

The sound of another bullet struck the truck, followed by a third one. The truck veered toward the ditch on the side of the road. Cole fought for control. "Hold on! The tires on the right side of the pickup blew out." *And I'm going sixty-five miles an hour.*

The deep trench loomed closer.

"Get up, Alexia!"

In the couple of seconds he had, he couldn't keep his truck on the highway. He gripped the wheel harder as the truck plunged into the ditch bordering a field of blooming flowers. The front end of his Chevy smashed into the side of the trench, stopping its progress.

The airbags exploded, hitting his chest with enough force to knock the air from his lungs and dispelling white dust into the cab. He coughed as he drew in deep breaths of the powder and turned toward Alexia, hoping she'd followed his last direction. He didn't have time to explain she should be upright in case the airbag deployed.

Plastered against the seat, she groaned but rolled her head toward Cole and gave him a reassuring smile. "I'm—okay."

"Good." He shoved his driver's door open. "Get down again and stay there."

"What are you going to do? The shooter's out there."

"I know, and I'm going hunting. Call Sheriff Woods and let him know what happened and where we are." After grabbing his cell phone in the console's cup holder, Cole reached behind the front seat and pulled out a rifle with a scope on it. "I have a handgun in my glove compartment. Get it for yourself." Then he low ran away from his pickup.

As Cole climbed out of the ditch seven or eight yards from his truck, he recalled the brief glance in the direction of the shooter. A tall, bushy tree in the middle of the field of pale blue flax seed was his target—if the assailant was still there. He wanted to take their attacker alive. When he'd been discharged from the army, he'd never wanted to kill another person—even an enemy, but he would protect Alexia at all costs, if it came down to that.

At the top of the seven-foot trench, he encountered the border of the blooming plants over two and a half feet tall. He sneaked into the field of flax, a nutty scent perfuming the air, and began crawling on his belly toward the tree about a hundred yards away. He was coming from the other side in hope of throwing the assailant off. From his vantage point in the tree, the shooter probably couldn't see Cole's pickup other than part of the very top of it. The guy wouldn't know if they were hurt in the crash or from the first shot he'd fired. Cole counted on that to pique the attacker's interest to find out and make him do something careless. As a sniper, Cole had learned to wait for the right opportunity.

Keeping his attention on the tree, he planted one elbow then the other, inching closer. He prayed cell reception was working out here, and Alexia could reach the sheriff.

One long second after another passed.

He froze when he spied movement in the tree. Suddenly a man dressed in camouflage dropped to the ground and sprinted in the direction of the truck, favoring one leg. Not wanting the shooter to reach Alexia, Cole leaped to his feet and shouted, "I'm here."

The assailant stopped, whirled around, and lifted his rifle at the same time.

Cole fired his gun a second before the guy pulled his trigger. The blasts rang through the field.

* * *

The need to know what was going on tempted Alexia to peek out the window, but she didn't. She held the gun in her hand, glancing at her watch for the tenth time to see how long it had been since she'd gotten hold of Sheriff Woods. Ten *long* minutes.

What was happening? Was Cole all right? Did this have anything to do with the other incidents? How in the world did the shooter know they would be in this spot? Had he been waiting for hours while they were in Great Falls? Questions continued to tumble through her mind with no answers.

Lord, we need Your help.

Another five minutes passed. When would the police be here?

Scrunched down in front of the passenger seat, Alexia tried to ease some of the aches from the tight place she'd folded herself. But her throbbing body continued to protest her position.

One shot followed immediately by another from the field above the ditch reverberated through the air. Alexia tensed.

That's it!

She couldn't sit here and wait for the shooter to come kill her. Without a vantage point for her to see him coming, he could easily approach the truck, jerk the door open, and fire point-blank before she could react.

She wriggled herself out of the hole she'd stuffed herself in. Her walking cast impeded her maneuvering effectively. She took twice as long to sit in the passenger seat, her gaze trained on the top of the ditch above the pickup.

How was she going to hoist herself up to the field?

* * *

The shooter in camouflage went down, dropping his weapon. Cole charged the man, searching in the flax seed plants for the man's rifle.

"Unless you want me to shoot you again, I'd freeze." Cole said only about three yards away from the assailant. When he stood over the guy, he leaned down and snatched his rifle. "You won't be needing this anymore, especially where you're going."

The wounded shooter tried to rise. He winced and sank back onto the ground. "I'm not telling you a thing."

"Not a wise decision. You've been caught shooting at us. That's attempted murder."

"I was target practicing."

Cole laughed. "That's a good one. So that's what you're calling my truck—a target. Sure it wasn't the people inside?"

The assailant pressed his lips together.

Sirens sounded in the distance.

"In case you think you'll be let go, think again. My truck has three bullets in it that will match the bullets from your weapon. With that and my testimony that you shot at me, you'll be in jail a long time."

The shooter glared forward, avoiding eye contact with him as Cole called for an ambulance.

Although he didn't appreciate his truck being shot up, Cole hoped this would put an end to what had happened to Alexia and the other employees during the past week.

He studied the man's face, trying to remember if he'd seen it on one of the videotapes he'd looked at this morning. The assailant was of average height, short brown hair, and a plain face. Nothing about him stood out that would make a person remember him.

Finally, two sheriff's cars pulled up and parked near where his pickup went off the road. He was surprised at the number of cars that had passed on the two-lane highway and hadn't stopped. A few had slowed down, but no one had checked to see if they needed help. He was glad they hadn't, but it was odd…unless—

He grinned. Alexia—not following what he'd asked her to do—to stay in the truck. When he'd left his vehicle, his focus had been totally on stopping the shooter. For once, he was happy she hadn't because he hadn't thought about passersby, stopping to help. The other side of the ditch hadn't been as tall as the one leading up to the field, and people would have seen the top half of his Chevy. He was thankful the road wasn't heavily travelled. Someone else could have been hurt.

Sheriff Woods climbed from the ditch, glancing over his shoulder and saying loud enough that Cole heard, "He's fine. It's the other guy on the ground."

Sheriff Woods and a deputy strolled toward Cole. "You had Alexia worried. She heard two shots but didn't know what happened."

"I assume she wasn't hiding in my truck."

The sheriff shook his head, gesturing toward his deputy to secure the shooter. "Nope. She tried to climb up the side of the ditch, but she didn't make it. She's covered in mud and isn't too happy that she'd been worrying about you for the past ten minutes." A more serious expression descended on Sheriff Woods' face. "What happened here? Alexia said you two were heading back to Moose Creek when someone shot at you, disabling your truck. You got out to go after the assailant."

"And I found him. He'd been shooting from that tree," Cole pointed toward a large one in the middle of the field, "and decided to see what happened after we ended up in the ditch. I think he had visions of finishing us off. He would have killed Alexia if she hadn't bent down to get something from her purse at the exact time the first bullet hit my truck."

Thank You, God, for protecting Alexia.

"This could be the guy that shot Becca Norman. I'd love to wrap up that case and be able to tell Red the trouble's ended."

"I agree. I was trying to remember if I saw him on the video I looked at this morning."

"I'll have a deputy go through all of the tapes again. I'm sure you two have had your fill of watching them. At least we can hold the man on attempted murder."

Cole decided he'd go through all the footage that had been gathered at Crescent City, too, probably not before going to the Flying Red. He hoped he could find the guy on one of those tapes. He glanced at the culprit on the ground. The deputy had him handcuffed and was tending to his leg wound until the paramedics arrived.

Cole handed the sheriff the shooter's

weapon then started walking toward the road. "Can we hitch a ride back to Moose Creek?"

"Sure." He cocked a grin. "As soon as I put a blanket down for Alexia to sit on."

"She's that bad?"

"Yep. Standing on her good leg, she grasped a small scrub growing out the side of the ditch. She was using it to hoist herself up. It didn't hold, and she slid down."

When Cole reached the edge of the field, he peeked down into the ditch and laughed. Sitting in the passenger seat of his pickup, Alexia looked at him, mud smeared down her front. The vision lifted his spirits.

* * *

The next morning at the diner, Alexia sat across from Cole, who had finished telling Charlie about what happened the day before. "I'm glad you thought it was funny. I was ready to come to your rescue if you needed me, and all I got from you was laughter." She swiveled her attention to Charlie and glared. "And you'd better not say a word. For all I knew, there'd been a shootout and both of them were dead."

"In that case, you could have waited for the sheriff and saved yourself the trouble of trying to crawl up an almost ninety-degree angle with a big black boot on your leg." Charlie took the last gulp of his coffee and reached for the pot to refill his to-go mug.

"Don't you have work to do, so we can leave in the next hour for the ranch?" Alexia asked, still remembering the fear she'd experienced when she'd heard those two gunshots in the field. Not knowing if Cole was alive or dead drove her to climb the side of the ditch until she'd pulled the scrub out and fallen backward with the bush clutched in her hand.

"Yes, ma'am. Then I'll pick up Cole's truck and go to Great Falls to pick up Becca." Charlie stood. "I've never been so glad to return to the Flying Red as I am today. See you two at the rodeo grounds."

"We won't be long. We'll be swinging by the sheriff's office first."

After Charlie left, Cole placed some dollar bills on the table.

Alexia pushed the money back toward him. "I'm paying. You saved my life. That's the least I can do."

"Have I convinced you now that whoever is behind this is after you? We need to look at people you, or your father, might have angered. Good thing we'll have a two-hour trip today to discuss options."

"I don't want to ignore any viable ones, but why don't you think the shooter yesterday was the sole person behind the sabotage?"

"I'm being cautious. We've talked about it possibly being two people. The sheriff is tracking where this guy, who's telling the authorities his name is Dustin Jones, has been."

"His name is all they know about him? There are a ton of Joneses in Montana alone." Alexia rose from the café table.

"Sheriff Woods is circulating his photo and name throughout the state. If that doesn't produce something, he'll widen the scope of his investigation. Jones tried to kill three people."

"At least we have an answer to who went after Becca since the bullet she was shot with matched the one from his gun."

Cole went out first and scanned the area before holding the door for Alexia to leave the restaurant. "I wish Jones's pickup gave us more clues about where he's from. He might be a hired thug."

"Because the license plate had been stolen in Billings?"

"Yes, that's one reason. And I'm betting his name isn't really Dustin Jones. All the sheriff has is his fingerprints, photo, and the name he gave us. So far, the fingerprints aren't in any databases and no one has recognized him."

Cole drove Alexia's truck to the sheriff's office, letting her out at the front door then parking. When he joined her just inside the station, a deputy escorted them back to a viewing room and stayed with them.

"When will the interrogation start?" Alexia asked, glad there was a glass mirror between her and the shooter. What little she saw of him yesterday had been enough to realize she didn't know him. The idea that someone could have hired him unnerved her more than she cared to acknowledge.

"Soon, ma'am. We're waiting for the state-appointed attorney for the suspect. When he requested one last night, that shut down his interview until one could be provided. Sheriff Woods wants everything by the book."

While the deputy hung back, both she and Cole faced the two-way mirror when the door in the interrogation room opened. The man, probably about thirty, stared right at the mirror as if he could see her watching him. Chills flashed up her arms.

"I know I asked you yesterday, but have you ever seen him around?" Cole repeated while holding her hand.

Alexia studied the man. Cole had called him average—a person who faded into a crowd, and she had to agree. Brown hair. Maybe five foot ten. Plain looking. Perfect for a hitman. Had he been paid to shoot at them? Or was there something more to the reason he did it?

When the sheriff entered with an older man who must be the suspect's lawyer, Sheriff Woods gestured for him to take the chair next to Dustin Jones.

The attorney introduced himself to Jones then said, "I would like some alone time with my client before you question him." He glanced at the two-way mirror. "In a room without a way to listen in on the conversation."

The sheriff frowned and opened his mouth to say something, but Jones cut him off, saying, "I don't need to talk alone with my lawyer. I'm not answering any questions. I'd like to go back to my cell." The shooter again looked directly at the mirror, his eyes narrowed—menacing.

"Very well." The sheriff went to the door and asked the deputy outside in the hall to escort the prisoner back to his cell.

Alexia sighed, watching Jones rise with the use of a crutch and make his way into the hall. Something about the way he walked nagged at her. He dragged the foot of his leg that hadn't been shot. The homeless guy in Crescent City had walked funny. The composite had been similar to Malcom Snyder, but Charlie hadn't thought it was Malcom.

"We might as well go to the rodeo grounds." Cole still held her hand and squeezed it gently. "He may change his mind later. I'm sure Sheriff Woods will keep us informed."

In the corridor, the sheriff and the suspect's attorney finished talking.

The lawyer disappeared down the hall.

"We discovered how Jones knew where you two were going to be." The sheriff joined Cole and Alexia.

"How?" Cole asked.

"There was a tracker placed on your truck. He didn't have to follow you. Jones must have watched and waited from his perch for you to come by. Hawkins called me this morning when he found it while he inspected your vehicle to see what needed to be repaired. I'll keep you two informed concerning this case. When it goes to trial, you both will need to come back to testify."

"Thanks, Sheriff Woods. I'm sure Dad will be calling you to offer his own thanks as well."

Sheriff Woods walked with them to the front door and shook their hands. "We'll keep trying to find out why he did this and who might be connected. I'll let you know if we discover anything. If you figure out anything that would help us with this case, please call me."

"Will do." Cole went outside first and held the door for Alexia while panning the surroundings.

"You think I'm still in danger?"

"Until proven otherwise, yes."

This was real. She was in danger and didn't know why.

EIGHT

Cole slanted a look at Alexia, asleep before they were ten miles outside of Moose Creek. He wasn't surprised. She'd been up a good part of last night. It had been hard for either one of them to go to bed after the attack yesterday afternoon. They had discussed everything happening in the world but nothing in their personal lives—not even the case.

He didn't think Jones was acting alone. If he'd been hired to do the job, it would have been to his benefit to talk and make a deal with the sheriff, which meant he somehow had a personal connection. But Alexia had no idea who he was and neither did Red or Charlie. He'd sent the photo of Jones to them and both had texted him back that they didn't recognize the man. At the ranch, he intended to show the picture to all the employees. He wanted to see their reactions to the mug shot. Jones might be tied to someone at the ranch or a fired employee. The key was to find out who the man really was. Sheriff Woods had good resources to track down that information, but Michael had connections throughout this part of the country, too. His cousin, Michael Knight, as well as the law enforcement officers in Crescent City and Moose Creek, were investigating the shooter's identity.

The problem was Alexia and Red might not have time on their side. The attacks had increased in frequency and intensity. He didn't want anything to happen to anyone else—but especially to Alexia. When he left the courthouse after their divorce proceedings, he'd been angry, hurt, and broken. He should have found a way to reach her, but he had nothing left inside of him to give her.

Again, he slid his glance toward his ex-wife. Her gaze coupled with his, and he smiled, warmed by the expression in her eyes. "It'll be better when we get to the Flying Red. Your dad might be a tough boss, but his employees respect him. You're familiar with the layout of the ranch and everyone around you. That'll help."

"Part of me is eager to get home, but the other is very aware of my father's disappointment. The last couple of calls he hasn't said much about how he feels. Probably because Mom was nearby. She has her hands full keeping him calm. Dad doesn't work that way."

Cole chuckled. "True, though in the past, you two usually worked well together. You're the yin to his yang."

"That's because I learned quickly how my father works in order to anticipate what I need to do. But for several years, I haven't been successful like before."

"What happened?"

When Alexia remained quiet, Cole knew the answer—Daniel's death and their divorce—topics they had avoided since they started working together. They couldn't anymore. "Since our son died, and we divorced?"

She nodded. "Dad had visions of Daniel eventually running the company and the ranch. He was the son he never had."

"He was one year old."

"A couple of times when you were gone, Dad flew us up to Montana so Daniel could get used to the ranch. And our son loved going, especially to see the animals. The last time, Dad took him on a horse ride. Daniel laughed and smiled the whole...way. He was going—" Her raspy voice faded into silence.

"Going to be a cowboy?" Cole glanced at Alexia.

Tears filled her eyes. "Yes."

"No one is more upset than me that I couldn't get back until a week after Daniel's death." Although he'd told her that three years ago, Alexia hadn't really listened to him. "I'm sorry, Alexia. I let you down when you needed me the most. One day, I hope you'll be able to forgive me."

Again, silence hung in the air for a long

moment.

"I hope you'll forgive me, too. We didn't support each other when we should have."

He smiled. "I agree. We've known each other for more than half our lives. I don't want to lose that connection. We aren't the same people we were in high school, but if nothing else, I want to be a friend." His grin grew. "Even if we live two hours away from each other. That's nothing in Montana."

She chuckled, her shoulders relaxing along with the tension between them.

Cole slowed Alexia's truck as they went through a small town, not too far from the ranch.

"We haven't talked about the case any. We were supposed to, but frankly, avoiding it for a couple of hours was nice," Alexia said.

"You needed to sleep. We'll have time at the ranch."

"How about you? You were up when I was last night." The rest of the tension in her body seemed to drain out.

"But I function on less sleep than you

do."

"Part of your training?"

"A survival technique."

"I don't think I can even fathom what you've gone through as a soldier."

"That's behind me."

One of her eyebrows arched. "Is it?"

"Okay, it's a work in progress. I've come a long way since I left the army."

"I wish I could say that. I feel like I've taken one step forward and two backward. Dad and I have always had a unique relationship, but Daniel's death hit him, and me, hard." She paused, rubbing her hand across her forehead. "He blames me for the fire."

"He said that to you?"

"No, but I heard Mom and him talking about it when I came back to the ranch."

"So, you've never talked to him about it?"

"I've avoided talking about Daniel's death even with Mom. I was afraid to see the disappointment in their faces."

"From what I heard, the firefighters had to carry you out of the house and watched to make sure you wouldn't try to go back in when their fire chief called all his guys out. The house was gone with no way to reach Dan—Daniel." His shaky voice stumbled over his son's name, his throat tightening.

"I fell asleep on the couch downstairs from exhaustion, and when I woke up to the fire alarm going off upstairs, it was too late. I tried to get up the stairs but couldn't make it to the second floor. Fire was everywhere. I ran back down the stairs, called the fire department, then tried again to get to Daniel. One of my neighbors had already called the firefighters. They came into the house. As they forced me outside, there was an explosion upstairs and the fire was completely out of control. All they could do was try to save the homes around ours. I've tried to forget that night. I can't. Everything else afterward was a blur."

"I have memories like that." Ones he wouldn't share with her. She didn't need to relive the horrors of war. He never wanted to. Before she asked him about his nightmares, he added, "You did what you could."

123

"There was smoke and even fire downstairs. Why didn't the fire alarm on the first floor go off? I tested it and the one upstairs every month."

"I'm going to say it again. You did what you could." Cole drew in several deep breaths. "You aren't the only one who blames yourself for not saving Daniel. If I had been home at the time, maybe I could have gotten to him in time. But I…" He couldn't seem to get enough oxygen into his lungs.

Alexia's hand clasped his arm. "No matter what we say, it won't change what happened."

"I should have been there for you. I would have been if I'd known."

"I know that now. I probably did three years ago, but the only thing I could see was my own loss and pain."

"We'd grown apart. I was gone so much."

"When we needed each other the most, we didn't know how to talk to each other."

That was his fault. With each mission he'd gone on, he communicated with her less and less. He couldn't share the part of his life he needed to with her. "We made mistakes, but Daniel never was one. I wasn't there then, but I am now. I'm not going to let anyone hurt you. I won't leave until I'm satisfied the case is settled."

She smiled. "I could get used to you being around. So could Dad. He did tell me that he didn't understand why we got a divorce. According to him, you were the best thing that happened to me."

"I have to admit it will be nice seeing your mom and dad again." He'd loved his parents, but he had been closer to the Richards than he'd been with them.

Alexia glanced at the clock on the dashboard. "You will in half an hour."

"Remember, I'm here for you even as a referee with your father." His gaze connected with hers. Michael asking him to take over the case had been the best thing that had happened to Cole in a long time. In the midst of all the nightmares he dealt with, a seed of hope planted itself in his heart.

* * *

As thirty minutes ticked down, Alexia prepared herself for the hundreds of questions her dad would bombard her with the second she exited her pickup. She still didn't know why the person had sabotaged RRR's events. "Dustin Jones" was involved, but she couldn't say he was acting alone. At least they had a little time before RRR headed back out with a series of rodeos and county fairs. Summer, only a few weeks away, would be busy for the company, when they made most of their revenue.

When the convoy of trucks and cars turned into the ranch, knots tangled together in her stomach. She was glad they were the last vehicle. Like Cole earlier, she needed to drag in deep breaths. She didn't know how else she could have handled the situation other than end the road trip before going to Moose Creek. Her dad wouldn't hear of it. In his defense, people in Moose Creek were counting on them to be there, and the shooting didn't occur until the last stop.

While the rest of the vehicles drove to the barn nearest the house, Cole parked in front of the sprawling, two story, ranch-styled house that had been added on over the years the family had owned the property. Originally, there had been one wing. Now there were two more. Her dad had added those in anticipation of having a lot of children. But after Alexia was born, her mother couldn't have any more babies. Each time she went by the unoccupied bedrooms, Alexia was reminded that she was the only child, and she'd lost her only child.

The front door opened, and her father emerged with her mother next to him. Dad's stoic expression only reinforced the feeling that the future of the Richards family weighed her down at the age of twenty-seven.

"You aren't alone, Alexia. I wasn't there for you three years ago, but I'm here now."

"Thanks, and I have forgiven you, Cole. You weren't given a choice by the army when you'd return home." She started to open her door, but Cole grabbed her hand and stopped her.

"Thank you. We can be an unstoppable team when we work together. Whoever is doing this better watch out." He smiled and lifted her hand, kissing the back of it.

With her cheeks warm, she glanced toward her father ascending the steps. "You know you're giving Dad false hope."

Cole's eyes widened. "Am I?"

For the first time in a long while, she wondered if they could at least be friends like they used to. She hoped so, but at the moment, she had to deal with her dad.

NINE

Alexia stared at her father making his way toward her at a slower pace than his usual one. A pasty white pallor painted his cheeks. His tan from working outdoors had faded, and he'd lost weight in the twelve days she'd been gone. His appearance hammered home that he wasn't recovering as fast as he'd declared he would, as though whoever was trying to hurt RRR knew her dad was vulnerable and wanted to make the situation even worse.

Stepping forward, she forced her worry to the background and smiled. "It's good to be home."

Her dad stopped in front of her, glanced

down at her cast, and lifted his arm as if he was going to hug her. Instead, he dropped it against his side. "Was the trip back here uneventful?"

"Yes. No problems."

After her mom hugged Cole, she stopped next to her father and scooped Alexia into an embrace. "I'm glad you're here." She gave Alexia an extra squeeze before moving back. "How's the ankle doing?"

Her mother's warmth replaced her dad's awkwardness. "Protesting when I have to be on my feet a lot."

"Then let's get you inside and settled. I've prepared lunch for you two." Her mom hooked her arm through Alexia's as Cole and her father shook hands. "Your favorite."

"Homemade chicken noddle soup?"

"Of course. Whenever you were sick or something was wrong, it always perked you up."

While Cole stayed back with her father, she and her mother headed inside. She waited until the door was closed then asked, "How's Dad really doing?"

"I'm thinking of roping him to his lounge chair."

"Maybe the more appropriate question is how are you doing?"

"I'm going to need a *long* vacation—without Red—when he recovers."

The impish gleam in her mother's eyes caused Alexia to chuckle. "I'm glad to see you still have your sense of humor. I know what's been happening on the road hasn't helped you to keep him from stressing."

Entering the kitchen, her mom waved her hand in the air. "I've given up on that. I told him the other night he had to make the decision to take care of himself. I can't force him, and I'm not going to try anymore."

"Mom! I can't believe you told him that."

"I should have done it years ago. He's been better the past couple of days." She carried plates and bowls to the table and set them on the placemat. "Your dad has been looking forward to seeing Cole. It was a nice surprise when he found out Michael couldn't do the job and was sending him. In fact, part of the reason Red's been calmer even with the escalating incidents is Cole. They talk several times a day. He's keeping Red advised."

"So was I." Alexia pulled open a drawer, gathered the necessary utensils, then put them beside the dishes.

"Your father has to feel he's in control even if he really isn't. His heart attack scared him, although he'd never admit it. Before that, he thought sheer force could accomplish anything. This past month has been an eye opener for him. I want you to become more involved in running the company even when he's recovered so we don't have a repeat of what happened to him. He has to slow down."

"Good luck trying to get him to do that."

"He hasn't gone to his office at the barn more than a few hours the past couple of days."

"Really? Are you sure he didn't sneak out to it?"

"Yes, because I've had Hank come up to

the house each evening and go over what occurred during the day." Her mother peered at the door leading into the hallway then leaned close to Alexia. "He doesn't know yet that two venues have cancelled our shows next month."

"When did this happen?" She'd hoped their problems wouldn't affect their business, but she wasn't surprised. Their shows and rodeos were a family event with lots of children attending.

"Yesterday after the shooting in Moose Creek. One was for the big Fourth of July celebration in Billings. The other was the opening entertainment for a rodeo."

"You can't keep that from him, especially the Fourth of July one. That's a two-day event."

"I want you to handle it. See if you can convince them to keep us, especially since we've discovered who's behind the incidents. Point out to them that the shooter was caught and is in jail."

"I may not be able to change their mind, Mom, but I'll call both places later this afternoon."

"Good."

Footsteps against the hardwood floor echoed through the house.

"How did you get Hank to keep quiet about the cancellations?" Alexia whispered.

"I told Hank I'd fire him if he told Red any bad news without running it by me first."

Surprise flittered through Alexia. "Hank's your brother."

"And should know better."

Alexia laughed. Hank, the ranch foreman, and her mother were twins. They could finish each other sentences.

While Cole and her dad came into the kitchen, Alexia helped her mom bring the serving dishes to the table. As she placed the soup tureen near her mother's seat, Cole's gaze captured hers and held it for a heart-stopping moment. No one else seemed to be in the room but them. She could remember a time when they used to complete each other's thoughts. But that was a long time ago. They could never go back to that life.

* * *

After lunch, Cole left the house for the main barn so that he could talk with Hank. He and Charlie were trustworthy and had been at the Flying Red Ranch the longest. He wanted Hank's take on what happened on the road. He was even more attuned to the people who worked here than Charlie.

He scanned the landscape with a range of mountains to the west. A gentle wind carried the scents of cattle, horses, and grass. The smells and sights surrounding him brought back good memories of his time here. He'd felt a part of the family even before he and Alexia had married. Cole's dad had died when he was young, but Red had become a surrogate father, showing him how to break a bronco, ride a bull, and many other things to run a ranch. When he'd completed his service in the U.S. Army, he and Alexia had planned to return to Montana and buy a ranch nearby. He'd already had several places in mind.

But their plans changed with Daniel's death.

No, that wasn't totally true. He'd changed before that. The carefree and open person he'd used to be died on the battlefield. He was working to get back to that guy, but he would never totally be like that again. Alexia had fallen in love with that man—not the one he was now.

Cole paused at the entrance into the barn and took one last look before stepping back into the place where he'd spent much of his past life—when he was young and innocent.

Hank came out of the tack room and headed in his direction. "It sure took you a long time to return here." Alexia's uncle shook Cole's hand then hugged him, slapping him on the back several times. He stepped back. "You're looking good. I'm glad you're helping Red."

"And that's why I'm here, to talk to you about what's been going on while I was gone."

"You mean who has a grudge against Red and his company?"

"Yep. Charlie told me about Malcom Snyder, Don Chambers, and Buddy Wills. I thought I might see Wills in Moose Creek at the rodeo, but he wasn't there."

"I heard he's moved to Nevada, and although Red fired him, he wasn't too upset about it. He'd been talking about moving to Las Vegas for a while. I saw his mom in town a few weeks ago, and she said he's happy there. The other two men could have let Bulldog out or stolen the petty cash. But hurt someone? I don't see it."

"Bitterness can infect anyone and change them."

Hank cocked his head and stared at Cole. "Are you talking about yourself?"

Stunned by the question, he sank down onto the edge of the desk. Was he?

"You lost your son. You might not know that I had a daughter, who if she were alive, would be about your age."

"I didn't know."

"Not surprising. I don't talk about her. That's how I dealt with her death for years. She died from meningitis when she was three. Martha and I never had another child. Karen's death nearly destroyed our marriage, and things were never the same after we buried her."

"Does Alexia know about your daughter?"

"No, I didn't—"

Cole heard a noise and swiveled his attention to the office entrance. Alexia came inside and shut the door.

"Why didn't you tell me, Uncle Hank?"

"Because my way of dealing with my daughter was not to talk about her. Just like you dealt with Daniel, and now I'm seeing the danger of holding your feelings inside." Hank cleared his throat. "Martha and I did everything we could to save our daughter but not even the doctors could. It happened so fast. But that didn't stop me from blaming everyone, including myself."

Alexia's eyes grew round. "You didn't cause the meningitis."

Hank glanced from Cole to Alexia. "And you didn't cause the fire."

Alexia sucked in a deep breath and stepped away.

"Helen told me she thinks you blame yourself for not saving Daniel. Sometimes there's nothing we can do no matter how much we want to. These past few years, I've watched you struggle to pull your life together."

"Why are you talking to me now?" Alexia moved back until the closed door stopped her.

"Because Cole's here. You two have a chance to come to terms with Daniel's death together now. Don't make my mistake and hold onto the bitterness and anger for years. After I talked with your mother, I went home, and Martha and I finally had a heart to heart about losing our daughter twenty-five years ago. I don't want you to wait that long—or never do it. You owe the other that. You two were meant for each other. Cole, I saw that the first time you came to the ranch."

Cole's throat swelled with emotions he'd kept suppressed for too many years. He glanced at Alexia, whose eyes shone with unshed tears.

Hank headed for the door. "Stay and talk. I have work to do. And, Cole, I'll think about who might have a grudge against Red and let you know if I come up with anyone."

Alexia shuffled to the side so her uncle could leave.

The sound of the door shutting closed again resonated through the office. Cole and Alexia stared at each other. He couldn't think of anything to say, and from the stunned look on Alexia's face, she couldn't either.

A tear leaked from her eye and ran down her cheek. His heart twisted. When he came home after Daniel's death, she never cried once or rather she'd never let him see her mourning their son, but he'd seen her red eyes.

She opened her mouth to say something but didn't. Another wet track ran down her face. In three steps, he stood in front of her. The urge to wrap his arms around her was overwhelming. When she looked down as though to hide her tears, he enveloped her, pressing her against him.

She laid her head against his chest and cried. Each sob tore at his defenses. He wanted to take her hurt and sorrow away, but he didn't know how. He couldn't even deal with his own. His tears blurred his vision, and he tightened his hold on Alexia.

"Uncle Hank is wrong. It was all my fault, Cole. Daniel is dead because of me."

TEN

Alexia relished Cole's touch. He leaned back, cradling her face between his large hands. His features came into focus through the sheen of tears. Anguish carved deep lines into his face.

"Let me help you, Alexia. If you can forgive me for not being there, you can forgive yourself for surviving the fire."

"I'm trying. I think I have and then the what ifs start. What if I'd fallen asleep upstairs in my bedroom instead of the couch. Or what if I'd heard the alarm quicker. Moved up the stairs faster. I just needed a couple of minutes."

"I've been there myself. All the what ifs

are speculations, and even if we had done them, there's no guarantee things would have turned out better. Do you think God wants us to forgive others but not ourselves? He wants the best for *all* His children. That includes you and me."

The deep ache in her heart demanded more. "Then why did He take Daniel?"

"I can't tell you that, but I do know we'll see Daniel again in Heaven. That's what we have to hold on to."

"It still hurts."

"Forgiving and forgetting are two different things. I had to forgive myself for surviving when some of my team died in battle, but I won't ever forget them. The same with Daniel. I should have been home to protect Daniel from the fire, but I wasn't."

"But I was."

He forked his fingers through her hair and cupped the back of her head. "I know, which makes it even worse. You were not to blame in any way. Faulty wiring was the cause." He drew her against him and entwined his arms around her.

With her ear pressed against his chest, she heard his strong heartbeat, a little fast, and savored the warmth of his embrace, as though he was trying to shelter her from the storm of grief. And she allowed him to do it. She cherished the bond for a few minutes while she struggled to let go totally of her anger at herself, Cole, and God.

"I wish we could have done this three years ago," she murmured.

"Neither one of us was in a place to really listen to the other." He kissed the top of her head and gave her a gentle squeeze.

A soft rap on the door finally broke them apart, and Cole reached around Alexia to let whoever was outside into the office.

Charlie came into the room, looking from Alexia to Cole. "Did I interrupt something?" A gleam danced in his eyes.

"No," Alexia said, but the tone of her voice mocked that answer.

Charlie held up a set of keys. "Hank told me you were in here. Here's your keys. The truck is running smoothly. The Moose Creek garage did a good job repairing it."

He plopped them into Cole's hand.

"How's Becca?" Alexia asked, putting distance between her and Cole before Charlie began asking more questions she wasn't ready to answer. Something just changed between her and Cole, but she didn't know exactly what it meant for them.

"Becca is doing okay for a lady who was recently shot. Her mom will be taking good care of her. I won't be surprised if she returns to work as soon as she can. She was thankful she was shot in the shoulder she doesn't use as much as the other when she does rope tricks. The last question she asked the doctor who released her was when could she go back to work."

"I appreciate you waiting for my truck. I didn't want Alexia driving hers alone."

Charlie smiled. "I didn't want her to be by herself either." He turned and moseyed toward the door. "See you both tomorrow." Then as he left, he closed the door.

Alexia moved behind the desk and sat. "I came down here to make a couple of calls. Mom told me before lunch that there have been two cancellations because of what happened in Moose Creek. Dad doesn't know. Only Hank and Mom."

"Are you going to tell your father?" Cole took the seat in front of the desk.

"Not until I've talked with both venues. I'm going to see if I can change their minds. It's not news I want to tell Dad, but we can't keep it from him for too long."

"Which venues?"

Alexia told Cole which ones. "They're willing to lose their deposit. We've done the Fourth of July Celebration in Billings for a long time. The other was a new one for us. Although it's much smaller than Billings, Dad was excited about the acquisition."

Alexia flipped through the Rolodex on the desk for the phone numbers for both places. "I was afraid we'd lose venues."

Cole rose. "Which means I need to go pay your competitor, Parker Franklin, a visit. How long are you going to stay down here?"

"A couple of hours. When Uncle Hank comes back, he'll fill me in on what's been going on."

"Then I'll come back here. While I think

you're safer here at the ranch, remember there may be someone still out to hurt you and your dad."

"But possibly not. Dustin Jones could have been working on his own."

"There's no connection between Jones and the company. We don't know who he really is. I showed your dad his photo, and he didn't know him, nor your mother. So what's his reason other than being paid for what he did?" Cole opened the door. "Hank's nearby. Stay here please."

"When have I not done what you asked?" Alexia grinned and picked up the receiver.

* * *

"So, what's this visit about, Mr. Knight?" Parker Franklin shook Cole's outstretched hand.

"I'm investigating the incidents that occurred recently concerning Red Richards' Rodeo Company.

The tall, lanky neighbor frowned. "What's that got to do with me? What incidents are you talking about?"

"The petty cash stolen from the RRR company in Silver Springs, the release of a bull to roam Crescent City, the cutting of a strap on a trick riding saddle, then, in Moose Creek, a couple of shootings." Cole held the man's gaze, refusing to look away first.

Franklin swung around and walked to a floor to ceiling window in his living room. "I'm offended. What kind of businessman do you take me for?"

Right before he'd arrived at the ranch, Alexia had called Cole to tell him about her conversation with the man in charge of the Fourth of July Celebration in Billings.

"A desperate one. You're in direct competition with RRR and losing the battle—that is until now. I understand you called the rodeo grounds in Billings first thing yesterday morning to inform them of the shooting, making sure to emphasize the danger to the audience. Then you lowered your price to do the show. Apparently, they informed you today, they've canceled the RRR contract and hired your company instead."

Franklin glared at Cole. "I didn't cause the problem, but I'm a businessman and know when I've been given a second chance. You can't prove otherwise. Leave before I have you thrown off my property."

"If you hired the shooter in jail in Moose Creek, I'll find out and be back with the sheriff."

Before the man could say anything else, Cole pivoted and strode out of the house, his hands clenched at his side. He'd call Sheriff Woods and see if there were any leads to the true identity of Jones. He'd have time to do some digging, too. Maybe Michael would be able to assist since he was staying close to home until Bella gave birth to their child. The last trip to the hospital had been a false alarm, but Michael was being cautious, as he should.

While he drove back to the Flying Red Ranch, thoughts of earlier with Alexia filled his mind. He hadn't felt that connected to her in several years. It wasn't just the death of Daniel that had driven them apart. His job had, too, or rather his inability to separate his personal life from his work.

When he pulled up to the house, he parked on the side near the garage closest to the barn and hiked toward it. Inside was deserted. Usually one or two employees were around. Cole knocked on the office door. No answer. He tried the knob. It turned, and he peeked into the room. Empty. Where was Alexia? Hank? She'd promised to stay put until he returned. He checked his cell phone, and as he'd thought, no call or text from anyone. He started to punch in her number when he glimpsed hers on the desk.

He didn't have a good feeling about this. His adrenaline began to pump faster through him. He jogged toward the back-double doors, partially open. He spotted a group standing around an animal on the ground in a pasture. He didn't know what was kept in that field.

As he hurried toward the men, Hank moved, and Cole spied Alexia with her uncle. At least she was safe, but something was wrong.

Alexia looked around Hank and caught

DEADLY FIRES

sight of him. She left her uncle and walked toward Cole. Her expression evolved from a sad to a furious one in the short distance between them.

"What happened?"

"I don't know. Keith found Bulldog collapsed on the ground. When Keith led him off the trailer earlier, the bull wasn't his usual mean-tempered self after traveling. In fact, Keith said he was sluggish. He came back after all the other animals were settled to make sure Bulldog was all right." Alexia waved toward the group. "He's dead."

"Any idea how?"

"No. I've called the vet. He's on his way. Bulldog was in good health this morning. No indication anything was wrong."

The hairs on Cole's nape stood up. "Make sure the vet determines how he died."

"Because you think someone did this to Bulldog?"

Cole nodded. "Where's the trailer he was transported in?"

"Stored at the west barn. We can use a three-wheeler. I'm coming with you." Alexia motioned for her uncle to join them. When he did, she said, "I'm going with Cole to look at the trailer Bulldog used. Let the vet know we need the cause of death as soon as possible."

On the ride, Alexia held onto Cole while he drove. "I'm not looking forward to telling Dad."

"I don't blame you. If this was foul play, then we know Dustin Jones didn't act alone."

"I know. I told the two venues that the shooter had been caught."

"He has. Just not the person behind him."

Cole pulled up to the west barn and glanced over his shoulder. "Whoever's doing this will be caught. I won't rest until he is."

Alexia climbed off the three-wheeler first. "Maybe we should look at the other places we're performing in the next month. I don't want anyone else hurt."

"That's an idea, but it'll hurt your

business."

"I realize that, and I doubt Dad will go for it. We go back out on the road in a week."

"Then we have a deadline to discover the culprit." As Cole made his way to the barn, he panned the area. No one in sight, yet he sensed they weren't alone. He inched closer to Alexia and put his hand on the small of her back. "Stay close."

"Jimbo should be here cleaning out the trailers and trucks."

When Cole pulled open the right side of the double doors, a creaking sound reverberated through the old barn.

"Normally the doors are locked so he must be here." Alexia entered first and called out Jimbo's name.

Silence prevailed.

Cole frowned and stepped in front of Alexia. "I should have brought my gun. It's in my truck. Stay behind me."

"I see Bulldog's trailer at the back," Alexia whispered close to Cole's ear.

Quietly and slowly, Cole crept past different vehicles used to haul the animals on the road. When he rounded the corner of the flatbed next to the bull's trailer, he came to an abrupt halt.

Alexia collided into his back. "What's wrong?" She peeked around Cole and sucked in a breath. "Oh, no!"

When she charged around him, Cole grabbed her arm and stopped her. "Don't!"

ELEVEN

Cole stared at a young cowboy lying on the ground and maneuvered around Alexia. "I'll check him. Call 9-1-1."

He glanced around the barn, wishing, again, that he'd brought his gun. From now on, he'd wear it all the time, because most likely, Jones's partner was among them at the ranch, possibly still nearby. Cole checked the man's pulse, spying a wound on the other side of his head. "He's been knocked out; he's unconscious. But he's breathing. Also call Hank to come here."

Alexia finished talking to the 9-1-1 operator. "That's Jimbo," she said to Cole then connected with Hank. "Cole and I are at the west barn. Jimbo's been hurt. We need you immediately, and bring the rifle from the office." She paused then added. "At the moment, we're fine. The sheriff and an ambulance are on their way."

When Alexia ended her call to Hank, she came to Jimbo's side and knelt next to Cole. "Why did someone do this?"

Cole glanced at the trailer Bulldog had been in earlier. "It might have something to do with Bulldog's death." He rechecked Jimbo's breathing and pulse. "Were there any physical signs that the bull had been shot or injured?"

"No. Keith said other than he wasn't his usual mean self physically, the trip back to the ranch went well. Keith always looks him over because once Bulldog kept ramming his head into the side of the trailer. He wanted out and was going to make a hole in the side so he could escape. That was when Bulldog was younger. As he'd grown older, he tolerated traveling better."

While the sound of a three-wheeler approached, Cole again made sure Jimbo's vital signs were still okay. When he pressed his fingers against the cowboy's neck, the man's eyelids fluttered.

"Jimbo," Alexia said. "Help is on the way."

The young man moaned and lifted his hand to touch his wound. His eyes opened. Then he winced, his hand dropping away from his injury. "What hap—pened?"

Alexia leaned over him so Jimbo could see her. "That's what we hope you can tell us."

Jimbo tried to sit up. "Hit—from behind."

Cole clasped his shoulders and gently pinned him to the ground. "Don't move until you've been checked out by the EMTs. They'll be here soon." The nearest town was twenty minutes away. "It's a good sign you've regained consciousness. Do you know who hit you?"

"No. Head—hurts. Light hurts eyes." The cowboy closed them.

Hank joined them. "Jimbo, this is Hank. I called your dad. He'll meet you at the ER."

Cole stood so Hank could sit next to the

injured man. "I'm going to check the trailer."

"I'll come, too." Alexia rose.

Cole paused at the entrance into the small trailer. Hay covered the floor. A metal trough hung on a wall. "I'll get a sample of the feed. Someone could have poisoned it."

Alexia moved further into the trailer, kicking some of the hay as though she were looking for something.

"What's wrong?"

"Where's the salt lick? Bulldog loves his."

"Maybe Keith or Jimbo removed it."

"Then why leave the feed in the trough?"

Cole shook his head. "I've read where a poisoned salt lick has been used to kill animals like deer and elephants."

Alexia folded her arms over her chest as if keeping herself warm. "We need to find out. We can't keep losing animals. We have to remove the salt licks until this person is caught."

"Alexia. Cole," Hank called out. "A deputy sheriff and the EMTs have arrived."

When Cole emerged from the trailer with Alexia right behind him, the paramedics rounded the end of a horse trailer. Hank stood and moved back to let them examine Jimbo while the deputy joined them.

"Deputy Carter, it's good to see you, but I wish it was under better circumstances." Hank shook the man's hand. "You know Alexia and this is Cole Knight."

"The sheriff is on his way. What happened?"

Cole explained about Bulldog, what he and Alexia found when they arrived, and their suspicions.

"You think this is tied to the sabotage at the rodeos?"

"Yes. One of the people involved in what happened on the road is in jail in Moose Creek, but so far, he hasn't talked. Sheriff Woods, who's overseeing the case, can fill you in."

"We received the photo and information about a Dustin Jones yesterday afternoon. We're looking into the young men in the

159

area. So far, he doesn't match anyone from around here. And no car in this county that fits the description of what he was driving has been reported stolen."

Cole exchanged glances with Alexia. "Do you mind if we show his photo around town?"

"No, but let us know if you find out anything."

"We will."

The EMTs had Jimbo on a gurney, but the young cowboy didn't want to go to the medical center.

"I'm gonna be fine." Jimbo struggled to sit up. "I've got work to do." With a pain-filled grimace, he sank back on the padding.

Alexia strode to the gurney. "Jimbo, whenever there's an injury at the ranch, our company policy is to have a doctor okay your return to work. Not a day earlier."

"Yes, ma'am."

She clasped his arm. "We'll be along to check on you. And your dad will be there."

Cole came up beside her as the

paramedics rolled the gurney out of the barn. "What's this about we'll be going to town?"

"He's one of our employees. I'm going to make sure he's all right, and I like the idea of showing the photo around town. I know some people who've been here a long time and know most of the people in the county."

"I don't want you leaving the ranch."

She waved her arm at the spot where Jimbo had been lying. Red darkened the dirt. "And I'm perfectly safe here? No one can get to me? I've been home a few hours and look at what's happened so far. I won't sit and twiddle my thumbs waiting for the person to do something else. I've got to work with you on this, or I'll go it alone." She lifted her chin a notch and stared at him.

He shook his head. "You're stubborn."

"That hasn't changed in our time apart. Dad can't fight this. But I can. Use your energy to keep him in the house and out of this."

He drew in a deep breath and released

it slowly. "Okay. But you have to do what I say. Not like you did in the ditch."

She nodded.

Her cell phone rang at almost the same time as Cole's. While she answered hers, he walked away and punched the accept button on his. "Is something wrong, Helen?"

"Red's beside himself. He glanced out the window and saw a deputy sheriff's car, the vet's van, and an ambulance. What's going on?"

Cole recited the events, starting with Bulldog's death. He glanced at Alexia as he talked and could tell her call was from her father. "Alexia and I'll come up to the house soon. Tell Red we're on the way. There's nothing he can do that isn't being done."

When he disconnected with Alexia's mother, Cole closed the distance between them and took the cell phone from Alexia in mid-sentence.

"Red, we're coming to the house." He pushed the off button.

Alexia's eyes grew round. "I can see his

blood pressure going through the roof."

"It sounded like he wasn't listening to you."

"Because he wasn't. I didn't have a chance to get past Bulldog is dead."

"Hank, finish up here. We need to go see Red." Cole took Alexia's hand and started for the three-wheeler.

* * *

Before Alexia could open the front door to the house, her father swung it wide, the scowl on his face underscoring how difficult the next half hour would be. She'd seen that look, which never boded well.

His large presence filled the entrance, a nerve in his cheek twitching. Her dad glared at Cole. "I have a right to know what's going on with my company."

"Yes, sir, and we're here to explain. It isn't a conversation to have over the phone."

Alexia made a decision: this was between her and her father. No one else. She pivoted toward Cole. "Fill Mom in. I'm going to talk with Dad." Then she swung back toward her father and slipped past him into the house. "I'll be in the den, Dad."

Without looking back, she marched in the direction of the room, the silence from the foyer unnerving. If she and her father were going to have any kind of relationship—personal or business—then something had to change. Not just for her but for her dad, too.

In the den, she planted herself in front of the fireplace and waited.

Long seconds ticked into a minute then another.

Her heartbeat thudded against her ribcage. Since she'd returned home after Daniel's death, she'd felt as though she were skating on thin ice, and that at any moment, she would fall into the icy water beneath her.

The sound of footsteps coming toward the den forced her to take in deep gulps of air. She wasn't even sure her dad would show up. It could be Cole instead.

But when her father appeared in the

entrance, she nearly wilted from holding her stiff posture for so long. She shored up her resolve and faced him, her arms at her side, her hands balled.

His gaze ran up her length and bored into hers. Tilting her head slightly, she didn't say a word but waited for him to come farther into the room.

Finally, he took several steps forward, peering at the couch nearby. "Have a seat."

She stiffened her spine even more. "No, I'm fine here."

He sighed. "I'm sitting, and I don't want to get a kink in my neck looking up at you." A long pause. "Please."

Her own weariness blanketed her. "Fine." She sat as he did at the opposite end of the sofa. "Dr. Roberts will run tests to see if Bulldog was poisoned. I suspect someone used his salt lick. It's missing from his trailer. Jimbo was cleaning the trailers out when he was hit over the head. We'll also test the feed that was left in Bulldog's trough."

"You think someone struck Jimbo and took the salt lick?"

"Possibly."

"Why take the chance?"

"Because whoever's behind this wants us to know we aren't safe. He wants to taunt us."

"That's what Cole thinks?"

"I don't know. It's what *I* think. We haven't had a chance to discuss it since it just happened."

Her father's features twisted into a scowl. "Do you, Cole, or the police have any idea who it might be?"

"If we did, I'd have told you. Our best lead is to find out who Dustin Jones really is. Before what happened to Bulldog, I believed there was a chance the man acted alone, but this latest incident has made it clear he didn't."

Her father struggled to his feet and began pacing. "It must be someone I fired."

"It could be a competitor like Parker Franklin."

He stopped and whirled toward her. "Anyone else?"

"Who have you made angry?" *Besides*

me.

"Even the men I've fired were given more than one chance to change. I pay the top wages in the area. I believe I'm fair to my employees."

But not to me. Why did you blame me for Daniel's death? Alexia gritted her teeth to keep those words inside. "I agree. Most of the people who work for the company have been here a long time. Maybe it has nothing to do with the ranch or the business."

"Personal?"

She nodded. All her suppressed emotions surrounding her son surged to the foreground. This wasn't the time to talk to her father about it. But then, when would be?

"I'm not a saint. I've made mistakes, but to go after my employees and animals..." He stopped at the fireplace and stared at the empty grate. "To go after my daughter..." He shook his head. "He should come after me." With his brow creased, he looked at her, a sadness in his eyes. "I'm sorry you've been caught in the middle of this."

Pain stabbed her heart at the anguish on his face and in his voice. She couldn't remember a time he'd apologized to her. She rose, wanting to go to him and comfort him. But something held her rooted to the floor. "You can't control what others do. I understand that, Dad."

Tell him.

His features morphed into a mask of anger. "He's a coward to go after you and others instead of me." He fisted his hands as though preparing for a fight.

"I don't want anything to happen to you, Dad. We'll find him and put a stop to all of this. You have to take care of yourself."

"I'm not an invalid. I don't need you to…" He snapped his mouth closed and slapped his palm against the mantel.

She hurried to him and stopped him from doing it again. "Don't. You're going to hurt yourself."

He looked away.

"Dad?"

He twisted around, his back partially

facing her.

"What's wrong? Should I get Mom?"

His shoulders sagged. "I should be able to protect you. That's my job as a parent."

His shaky words, so similar to the ones she'd thought when Daniel had died, inundated her with the helplessness she'd felt when she couldn't rescue her son.

"He could have killed you yesterday."

Trembles moved up her body. Alexia sank onto the stone fireplace, lowering her head, trying to dismiss the utter hopeless vulnerability she'd experienced—desperate to run back into the raging fire and get Daniel.

"Alex?"

The heat of that blaze hadn't even warmed the icy fear flowing through her veins. As the minutes ticked away, she died a little with the passage of time. She didn't even know how she ended up being taken to the hospital in an ambulance.

A strong hand clasped her shoulder. "Alexia, what's going on?"

The frantic urgency in her father's voice yanked her back to the present.

A sheen to his eyes, her dad sat beside her and slipped his arm around her. "I'm sorry you had to go through yesterday."

Tell him!

"That's not it."

"What do you mean? Of course, something like that would wreak havoc on anyone. If someone had shot at me—"

She leaped to her feet and hovered over him. "Why did you blame me for Daniel's death?"

TWELVE

Cole followed Helen into the kitchen.

"I feel like I need to go in and rescue Alexia," Helen said.

"Alexia can take care of herself."

"I know." Helen crossed to the pot on the stove. "Coffee?"

"Yes, please." After Helen joined Cole at the table and they sat, he asked, "What happened to Alexia and Red's relationship? She's always strived to do her best for him, and he'd expected that from her, but something's different now."

Helen sighed. "Since she returned to Montana, their relationship has been precarious. I've tried to get Alexia to talk.

She won't, especially about Daniel. She shut down, but I've seen something different since you two came to the ranch. Is she discussing Daniel with you?"

"We finally are. I was in the same place as she was. I locked the pain away. I couldn't express it to anyone, not even Alexia three years ago." Going into battle had been a way for him to deal with his anger over Daniel's death. And helping the locals who were suffering in a war-torn country gave him a reason to wake up each day.

"Then there's hope you two will get back together. It broke my heart when she divorced you. Red's, too. He couldn't understand it. We've always felt you both were meant for each other. You weren't just our son-in-law but our son."

The temptation to tell Helen about what was at the root of Alexia's problem weighed heavily on Cole, but it wasn't his place to do that. He hoped Alexia would finally work it out with her father. "And I appreciated that. I lost my own dad at a young age. Red easily fell into that role as Alexia and I began getting serious. When you and Red came back to Montana after Daniel's funeral, Alexia and I hardly talked to each other. I could have used Red at that time. The problem is, I didn't realize that talking about it with someone I trusted and respected could make a difference until I left the army last year."

"Alexia didn't want us to stay. Believe me I tried. We prolonged leaving at least for a few days after you returned from overseas." Helen covered his hand on the table. "Don't give up on her. You two should be together."

Cole wasn't sure about that. They'd both made mistakes and hadn't fought enough for their marriage.

"The loss of a child is a parent's worst nightmare. I didn't lose a child that had been born, but I did miscarry three times when Alexia was very young. We both wanted more children, but Red did even more than me. It didn't happen, though, and it nearly ended our marriage. We separated for six months. Alexia probably doesn't remember, but I returned home to stay with my parents during that time."

"How did you get back together?"

"Alexia missed her daddy. She was always talking about him. Then Red showed up at my parents' house and persuaded me to give him another chance. I couldn't resist him. It took a while after I returned to the ranch to mend our marriage, but we did and it became even stronger."

Maybe there *was* hope for Alexia and him. But until Alexia dealt with all the issues and forgave herself for Daniel's death, it wouldn't work.

* * *

Alexia stood before her father whose eyes widened and his mouth remained closed. "Dad, I need to know. Why did you blame me?"

"You heard what I said that day?"

"Yes, and I haven't been able to forget it since I did."

He inhaled a deep breath, held it for a moment, then released it slowly. "I should never had said that. I was so angry at God and everyone around for taking Daniel from us. Your poor mother got the brunt of it. I thought she would leave me again."

"Leave you? When did she do that?"

"When you were young. You were three. We were separated half a year. We had our attorneys working on the divorce."

Alexia couldn't believe what her dad was telling her. She dropped down beside him on the fireplace. "Why?"

"We tried to have more children. She miscarried each one. It put a great deal of stress on us. She felt it was her fault. I thought it was mine."

"Your fault?"

"My desire for a large family put a lot of stress on Helen, and with each miscarriage, the burden weighed even more."

Alexia remembered how she'd blamed herself for Daniel's death and Cole had blamed himself.

"The fault isn't either of ours. I finally realized it wasn't meant to be. Helen was and is the only one for me."

As she'd felt about Cole. "How did you come to that conclusion?" Had she turned away from the one person who could have helped her heal?

Again, silence pervaded the room.

Her father dropped his head and combed his hands through his silver gray hair. "I began seeing a woman in town."

"You dated!"

"More than that."

Shocked, Alexia couldn't think of anything to say.

"Your mother knows. When we decided to fight for our marriage, I told her everything about the affair with Marilyn Tyler."

A bolt of anger flashed through her. "What else aren't you telling me?"

"I'm sorry, Alexia. I've made many mistakes in my life. I'm lucky your mother forgave me. I hope you will."

She couldn't lie to him. She stood and started for the door. "I don't know if I can."

She left the den as fast as she could before she said something else to her father. He'd betrayed her mother! The thought made her hands shake. She needed to get out of the house. She went looking for Cole.

When she found him in the kitchen talking to her mom, Alexia couldn't look her in the eye, knowing what her dad had done. Her mother would know something was wrong, and Alexia didn't want to answer any questions. "We need to go check on Jimbo."

Cole pushed to his feet and kissed her mom on the cheek. "Thanks for the coffee and company, Helen. We'll probably be gone a few hours."

"Please keep us informed about Jimbo."

"We will, Mom."

As they walked from the house, Cole placed his hand at the small of her back, and Alexia didn't feel so alone. Her conversation with her father cleared up a few concerns, especially about thinking he blamed her for Daniel's death, but she'd had no idea about her parents' problems when she was a young child. She'd always admired their close relationship. The same with Uncle Hank and his marriage. What else did she not know about her family?

When Cole started her truck and drove

away from the house, he glanced toward her and asked, "How did it go with Red? Did you talk to him about what you overheard three years ago?"

For a few seconds, she didn't know how to answer Cole. Then she suddenly knew what she needed to do if she and Cole would ever have a chance to get back together. And in that moment, she wanted to—at least give it a try. They spent so many good years together as friends and lovers. She wanted to fight for their relationship.

She twisted to the side so she could look at Cole while they talked. "Have you ever thought you knew everything you could about a person, but you really didn't?"

"Yes—us."

She grinned. "Me, too, but besides our relationship."

"I've been disappointed with certain people I've dealt with in my life. What are you getting at?"

"I just discovered my father had an affair when my parents were separated and were filing for a divorce." The words tumbled out before she lost her nerve to share with Cole. She didn't want anything between them anymore. "I don't know my parents like I thought I did. They always seemed so happily married and to find out they weren't was a shock."

"How did you end up on that subject?"

"When I asked Dad if he blamed me for Daniel's death, he was so upset that I overheard what he said. He apologized and told me he'd been in a bad place at that time and taking it out on people he cared about."

"Do you believe he doesn't blame you?"

Alexia remembered the look of anguish on her father's face when she told him. "Yes, because I was in that place, too."

"How did you two end up talking about Red having an affair?" Cole halted at a stoplight on First Street in Red Butte."

"I always felt that Dad loved me, but he also wished he'd had a son. Actually, he'd wanted more children, not just a son. Mom had several miscarriages and found out she couldn't have any more babies. Dad didn't take the news well. It led to fights and accusations. I was three when it happened and don't really remember anything about it. After six months, he realized he needed to fight for his marriage. She'd moved to my grandparents' house in Missoula. He asked her to come back to the ranch."

"Does she know about the other woman?"

"Yes, and she's forgiven him." Alexia ran her fingers through her hair. "I was shocked. I never would have thought that of my parents."

"I imagine I didn't know everything about my parents either. Do you forgive your father?"

"He didn't do it to me. Only Mom."

"But you were affected once he told you the story."

"Yes, it did." Alexia thought about Cole's question. How did she feel? Her dad's affair was over twenty-four years ago. She remembered all the times through the years she'd caught her mom and dad kissing, holding hands, or hugging. "But now that I've thought about what he did, I have to forgive him. I don't want to carry that anger around with me. I'm glad they worked things out and became stronger because of the situation."

Cole pulled into a parking space near the medical center for Red Butte and turned toward her, taking her hand. "Then there's hope for us."

"I hope so."

He drew her toward him and leaned forward, his lips brushing across hers. When he deepened the kiss, she put her arms around his neck. She didn't want this to end. For the first time in years, she felt at home as he embraced her.

He pulled back when another car drove into the parking lot. "We have a lot to talk about after we catch the assailant."

She smiled. "Let's go see how Jimbo's doing. I know a few busybodies we can show the photo of the shooter. If he was in Red Butte–even visiting—they would know.

* * *

Alexia approached Mrs. Catwell's front

porch where she and two neighbors sat drinking iced tea. "Good evening, ladies." She gestured. "I'm sure you remember Cole Knight."

"Are you two getting back together?" Mrs. Catwell, gray-headed and five feet tall, asked, indicating the loveseat glider nearby. "Sit down."

Alexia learned to avoid answering too many questions about herself. Once she had when Mrs. Catwell and her best friend, Mrs. Smith, cornered her before her wedding. News quickly traveled around town about every detail of the wedding with embellishments like she was going to release hundreds of butterflies when they left the church. Several guests wanted to know when that was going to happen. They wanted to take pictures. "We're here because we need to identify a man in a photo. He's in jail for shooting at Cole and me yesterday."

"Oh, my! Shooting at you two." Mrs. Smith held out her hand. "Let's see it. We heard, Cole, that you were working on a case for Red. I'd love to help solve a crime.

Mysteries are my favorite type of books to read."

"Yes, I work for the Knight Investigation Agency now." He handed Mrs. Smith his cell phone with Dustin Jones's picture on it.

The bottle-produced red-haired woman studied it then looked up. "There's something about him, but I don't quite remember what." She passed it to Mrs. Catwell.

"I see what you mean. I've seen him somewhere."

Mrs. Byrd snatched the phone away, dug her glasses out of her pocket, and put them on. Even with them, she couldn't see much. "Who does he say he is?"

"Dustin Jones," Alexia said.

Mrs. Byrd held the photo at arms' length and tilted her head to one side, examining it with the only narrow vision she had. "Nope. I've never seen him."

Cole took his phone back. "Ladies, if you remember anything, no matter how little, please call me at this number." He withdrew business cards from his pocket and handed one to each woman.

"Shoot. I wanted to help. Maybe if you wait a little while, I can think of something. How about some tea?" Mrs. Catwell asked.

"We can't stay long, but I am thirsty." Cole reached and took the glass that Mrs. Catwell had already filled. "We've been asking people around town about the man in the photo."

"I'll take one, too." Her throat parched, Alexia drank several sips before she settled back on the glider and cradled the cold cup between her palms. She wanted to talk with Mrs. Byrd alone about Marilyn Tyler. Mrs. Byrd rarely spread any gossip around Red Butte, but she knew everyone in town. Too bad her vision had worsened in the past few years.

Mrs. Catwell stroked her chin and looked up toward the porch ceiling. "I think that young man has been in Red Butte before, but it was a while ago. He doesn't live around here."

"This will nag me until I think of where I saw him. When I do, I'll let you know." Mrs. Smith pocketed Cole's business card. "And he is in jail?"

"Yes. He can't hurt anyone now." Alexia didn't want the ladies to think they were in danger.

Snapping her fingers, Mrs. Byrd sat forward. "Let me see the photo again."

Cole showed it to her.

"I know where you and I saw him," Mrs. Byrd said to Mrs. Catwell. "He was carrying moving boxes out of my neighbor's house down the street."

"Ah, yes, Ed Tyler's place."

Alexia stiffened at the mention of the Tyler name.

Cole shot her a quizzical look before saying, "Do you remember when this was?"

"You're talking about when Ed Tyler died, and Marilyn packed up what she wanted then sold everything else." Mrs. Catwell smiled. "I remember that day. She arrived in town and left after only spending two hours in the house. Didn't even stay for Ed's funeral, but then I don't blame her. Ed disowned her, or so he told her. But since she was his only child, the estate went to her because he didn't have a will."

"I'm glad Marilyn got something. Ed

was a lousy father." Mrs. Smith sipped her tea.

"Do you remember the man's name?" Alexia wanted to ask so much more than that, but she didn't want Mrs. Catwell or Mrs. Smith to remember anything about her dad having an affair with Marilyn Tyler.

"I do," Mrs. Byrd said. "As you know, I lived next door to Ed. I heard Marilyn call him Rusty. I don't know his last name. I hope that'll help you."

Cole rose. "It will, ladies. Thanks, and if you remember anything else, please call me."

Mrs. Byrd stood at the same time Alexia did. "I'd appreciate you two walking me to my house. It's starting to get dark and my eyesight gets worse then."

"It's my pleasure." Cole offered her his arm.

Mrs. Byrd grinned from ear to ear and started down the steps with him.

"Thank you. Have a nice evening," Alexia said to Mrs. Smith and Mrs. Catwell then quickly followed Cole and Mrs. Byrd.

When they arrived at her house, Mrs.

Byrd took Alexia's hands, leaned close, and whispered, "If you want to know anything else about the Tyler family, I might be able to help you. We were neighbors for thirty years. Living next door, I saw things others didn't."

"Can you tell me anything about Marilyn?"

"She was very secretive and private. She lived with her father, but she made sure he didn't know what she was doing."

"Why did she leave town?"

"Ed kicked her out, but I think she would have left even if he hadn't."

"Why?"

"Just a feeling I had back then."

Alexia gave Mrs. Byrd a hug. "Thank you."

While Cole made sure Mrs. Byrd got inside her home safely, Alexia watched them, wondering if the Tyler's' neighbor knew about her father and Marilyn. If she did, Alexia felt confident she wouldn't say anything to others or she would have on the porch.

As they walked back to her SUV, Cole

asked, "Is Marilyn Tyler the woman your dad had an affair with?"

"Yes."

Cole opened the passenger door for Alexia. "Which means she could be behind this."

THIRTEEN

After working for hours the next morning, Cole punched his fist into the air. "Bingo!"

Across the room at her father's desk in the house office, Alexia looked up at him. "Did you find Marilyn Tyler's address?"

"Yes and no." When she pinched her lips together, he continued, "I found her last residence, but she died two months ago."

"Have we hit another dead-end?"

"Maybe. She moved from Missoula before her father died. Closer to here—in Blue Sky."

"That's only about two hours from here. I wonder if any of her family live in the area."

"I don't know, but I think it's worth driving to Blue Sky and asking some questions."

Alexia frowned. "Today?"

"Yes. This is the best lead to figure out who Dustin Jones really is. Is he Rusty who helped Marilyn after Ed died? Did our shooter come from Blue Sky? Once we find out his full name, Sheriff Woods may have some leverage to get him to talk. I've got to try. I feel like I'm sitting here waiting for the other shoe to drop."

She rubbed her hands up and down her arms. "I know what you mean. I'm not just concerned about who the assailant is, but will my father still have a company after all the bad publicity? The article in the Billings newspaper yesterday didn't do us any favors. I suspect the committee for the Fourth of July celebration will call me today and tell me it's not possible for us to take part in the festivities even with the gunman in jail in Moose Creek."

"But the quicker we get this solved, the less harm there will be to the company. I'll get Charlie or Hank to stay at the house while we're gone."

"I can't go. Dad wants us to work together to develop a strategy to keep the company in the black. This is the first time he's asked me to help him like that, but you need to go. Blue Sky might have answers for us."

Cole stood. "Not unless Charlie or Hank can be in the house. I don't want you all alone, especially here at the ranch after what happened to Jimbo."

She rose and crossed the room to stand near him. "The alarm system at the house is good."

"I know but—"

Alexia touched two fingers to his mouth. "You can't be in both places at once. I know how to defend myself. Remember all those times you took me to a firing range. I'll call Uncle Hank and have him come up for lunch and help Dad and I brainstorm a possible course of action for the company." She moved within inches of him and locked her hands behind his neck. "Your job is to find who's behind the sabotage. What's keeping you here?" She grinned. "You should be out of here and driving away."

A gleam danced in his eyes, and he bent his head closer. "Just as soon as I get a good-bye kiss, I'm out of here."

He wrapped his arms around her and pulled her against him, claiming her mouth in a deep kiss he'd kept bottled up with all his suppressed emotions for years. He'd missed her in his embrace with his lips tasting the sweetness of hers. Her scent of vanilla surrounded him, urging him to stay and see where this would lead. Before he surrendered to his needs, he dropped his arms and stepped back.

"I wish I could stay and see where this goes, but you're right. My priority is finding the assailant. I don't want to lose you when I just found you again. When the guy behind this is caught and the case is over, you and I have a date." He closed the space between them, clasped her upper arms, and left her with a hard, quick kiss.

"Call Hank now," Cole said as he walked from the office.

* * *

192

Alexia felt like she was floating on a white, fluffy cloud lazily drifting across the blue Montana sky with not a care in the world. The kiss she and Cole had shared a few hours ago still teased her thoughts and warmed her body.

"Alexia, what do you think about personally meeting with the people involved in the Fourth of July celebration?" her father asked, sitting in a chair across from her in the house office.

She was glad her father now knew about the cancellations. She didn't want to keep any secrets between them. "From how the manager sounded on the phone this morning, I don't think it would do us any good. But that doesn't mean we can't approach other venues personally. I have a tip about an event in Great Falls the weekend after the Fourth of July. Also, I've been thinking about us offering a rodeo camp in conjunction with the rodeo circuit for both adults and kids. Experience how to be a bull or bronco rider. Learn how to do a trick on a horse or rope a cow. Things like that. If we work fast, we could set some up for the last six weeks of summer at various places. Then if it's a success, do more of it next year. What do you think, Dad, Uncle Hank?" She glanced from one to the other, her breath bottled in her lungs.

"I love that idea. Sorta like a training camp for the rodeo." Her father smiled from ear to ear. "But none of this will work until we find who's sabotaging us. I'm going to believe the assailant will be caught, and we need to be ready. We can send out feelers about a rodeo camp and see who might be interested."

"We'll want to appeal to all the people who've been big fans of the rodeo but have never participated in one. Give them a feel of being in one." Alexia turned her attention to her uncle. "What do you think?" When he didn't reply, she leaned over and nudged him in the arm. "Uncle Hank, your thoughts?"

He chuckled. "Sorry, I was woolgathering how to do it, especially with only six weeks to plan. But I think we can if we start publicizing as soon as possible." He cocked a grin. "By the way, I think the idea is brilliant." Her uncle rose with his mug in his hand. "I'm going to check on

Helen. She may want to be in on this conversation. Does anyone want a refill of coffee?"

Alexia shook her head. She'd had enough. She hoped to take a nap this afternoon and try to catch up on sleep so she and Cole could have a long talk tonight when he returned from Blue Sky.

Her father gave Hank his empty cup. "Nothing beats Helen's coffee."

Hank chuckled. "That's why I come up here during the day to get some."

When Hank disappeared in the hallway, her dad cleared his throat. "Cole really thinks that Marilyn Tyler had something to do with our troubles?"

"Not necessarily with the sabotage, but she may have known the shooter. You know the guy whose picture I showed you yesterday."

"I haven't seen Marilyn in years, not since she moved to Missoula."

"She moved from there to Blue Sky a while back, but she died two months ago."

"Then why is Cole going there?"

"To see if anyone knows the shooter and talk to people who knew her. We think the guy's real first name is Rusty, but we need a last name. Then Cole and the police can dig into his life and maybe discover someone who was working with him."

"Or he's working for them."

"Yes. Maybe the person behind this hired him, or there could be a more personal connection."

Her father relaxed back against the cushioned chair and kneaded his nape. "I noticed how Cole's been looking at you lately. And you at him. Is there anything you have to tell me?"

She held up her hand. "Hold it right there. Cole and I are talking. That's it."

"Well, of course, you're talking. He's working on our case."

"About the past. There. That's all you're gonna get."

The biggest smile she'd seen on her dad's face in months transformed his expression. "Then there's hope, and I call that good news. You two have always been meant for each other."

Alexia pressed her lips together and looked down at the paper pad in her lap where she'd been writing notes of their meeting. She didn't want her father to be disappointed if nothing came of her talks with Cole. "We have a lot to plan and get started on. Where do you want to hold the rodeo camp?"

Her dad began rattling off town names, and Alexia jotted them down, glad to have something to do rather than think about Cole's trip. She prayed he came back with information that would help them find the person Dustin—Rusty—was working for.

* * *

Cole pulled up to a small, white clapboard house, with weeds and occasional patches of grass growing out of control in the front. The peeling paint and neglected yard made him wonder if anyone had lived here since Marilyn's death.

Only one way to find out. He climbed from his truck and strolled up the cracked sidewalk to the porch. To his right, a rocker sat, looking as though it had been neglected for months. Cigarettes overflowed from an ashtray on a small wooden table next to the chair. He examined them. The butts on top looked recent while the others underneath had been there for a while.

Maybe someone did live here.

Cole rang the doorbell. He heard the chimes sound through the house. When no one came to answer, he tried to open the screen door, but it was locked so he knocked on it. He moved to the left and peeked into the medium-sized window into a living room, tidy with no evidence anyone lived there currently.

He'd known this was a good possibility, but after circling the house and looking inside, he decided to pay the neighbors a visit. He didn't want to go back to the ranch without a lead or, at the very least, know for sure that Blue Sky was a dead-end.

He walked to his truck and glanced up and down the street. Withdrawing his cell phone from his pocket, he called Alexia. When she answered, his heartbeat sped up at the sound of her voice. He missed her.

He'd never stopped loving her.

Cole lounged against the side of his truck. "I'm not sure anyone lives at Marilyn's address. I'm going to talk to the neighbors and then call the sheriff. There's a café in the small downtown that looks like it's where people go to hangout. I'm hoping someone can ID the photo of Dustin Jones. How are things going at the ranch?"

"Good. No problems here. In fact, I made a suggestion to Dad about the company and we're working up a plan to implement it. I almost didn't say anything. He's usually set in his ways and not open to something new."

"I'm glad he did. It's time he realized it's a family business, and he needs to utilize you. Is your meeting over?"

"Yes. I know my dad isn't one-hundred percent when he stops to take a nap. I think I'll take one, too."

Cole glimpsed a young woman descending her porch steps across the street. "I need to go. A neighbor's come outside. I'll be back at the ranch in three or four hours. Stay at the house. Is Hank still there?"

"Yes, worrywart."

"That's because I don't want to lose you again. Bye." Leaving her with something to think about, he disconnected and pocketed his cell phone. The young woman glanced back at him then hurried even faster to her car.

"Ma'am, I just need to ask you some questions." Cole tried to catch her, but she sped away.

Standing in her yard, he looked around, trying to decide which place to go to first. He started on the right side of the young lady's house, knocking on the door. No answer. He kept going until he ended up at the home next door to Marilyn's.

As he approached, a gray-haired woman drove into her driveway, then headed toward her mailbox at the curb.

Cole stopped on the sidewalk. "Does anyone live there?" Cole pointed at Marilyn's house. "I was hoping to talk to the owner."

"Marilyn Tyler did up until two months ago."

"Do you know where she went?"

"She died. Her daughter comes by occasionally and checks on the house."

A daughter? "Is she going to sell the house? I'm interested in it."

The neighbor frowned and shrugged.

"Marilyn Tyler did everything she could for her daughter, but Kim always wanted more. I have no idea what she'll do with the house. As you can see, it's an eyesore. Marilyn never let it get so rundown."

"Does Kim live in Blue Sky?"

She shook her head. "And she hasn't been here in over two weeks."

"Where does she live?"

"Some ranch west of here."

"How old is the daughter?"

"In her twenties." The woman narrowed her eyes. "What's this about?"

Cole removed his wallet and showed the older woman his private detective license. "It involves attempted murder. I'm working with Sheriff Woods in Moose Creek on a case. I have a few photos I'd like to show you. If you know who the person is, please let me know." He'd taken pictures of everyone who worked for the company, not only those who'd been on the road. He flipped through them on his phone.

"That last one is Kim."

He slid the screen back one space. "This one?"

The neighbor nodded.

Marcie. "Have you seen this guy with Kim or in Blue Sky?" Cole held up Dustin Jones's photo.

"That's Rusty Nail, Kim's boyfriend. I met him at Marilyn's funeral. I won't forget that name. I once stepped on a rusty nail and had to have a tetanus shot. I hate shots."

"Does he live in Blue Sky?"

"I don't know. I'd seen him around the place before Marilyn died so he might."

Cole smiled. "Thank you for your help."

He quickly crossed the street, withdrawing his cell phone to call Alexia to let her know what he discovered. There was no answer at the house. He called the office in the barn. No answer there either. He texted her that it looks like Marcie was behind everything and that he was heading back. Something wasn't right.

An urgency prodded him to wrap up his time in Blue Sky and return to the ranch. He'd stop by the sheriff's office to let him know about Rusty Nail and for him to contact Sheriff Woods.

On the way to report Rusty, Cole placed a call to the sheriff in the county where the ranch was located. Bob Anderson was a friend of Red's, and if nothing else, he could alert them about Marcie since he would be driving in and out of a cell phone dead zone on his way back to the Flying Red.

* * *

After a long meeting with her dad and Hank, Alexia's recent sleepless nights had finally caught up with her. She'd hoped the nap would keep her sharp and ready to continue their conversation about how to keep the company afloat. When her eyelids lifted halfway, the urge to close them and get more rest enticed her to do just that.

What time is it?

Groggy, she rolled her head to the side and glanced at the bedside clock. Four o'clock! She'd slept longer than she'd intended. Why didn't her father or mother wake her? Maybe her dad was still asleep, and her mom decided to let them rest. It wasn't like they didn't need it since the sabotage began. The pull to return to sleep grew stronger. She fought it, but it felt as though ropes held her tied to the bed.

She looked down the length of her body. No ropes. If she didn't know better, she would think she'd been drugged. But all she'd drunk were two cups of coffee, made by her mother then right before her nap a cup of chamomile tea. She fought the cobwebs that clung to her mind and struggled to sit up.

Then she scooted to the side of the bed and rose, her mouth dry. With leaden steps, she made her way into the connecting bathroom and splashed cold water on her face. When she looked in the mirror, it seemed as if she was staring at a stranger. For a few seconds, lightheadedness attacked her, and she grasped the edge of the counter to keep upright. When it passed, she dampened a washcloth, held it up to her face, then filled a cup with water and drank it.

Cole should be back soon. He never called to let her know what he found out. She hoped that didn't mean he came up empty-handed. Maybe she slept through his call. She returned to her bedroom and reached toward the nightstand for her cell phone where she usually kept it when sleeping. It wasn't there. Had she left it in the office downstairs? Probably. It had been on the end table next to where she'd sat. With all that had been happening, she could have walked out of the room and not given it a second thought.

This was not the time to crash. She'd go downstairs and see if he'd called. She gripped the knob, turned it, and pulled. Nothing. She tried to open the door again.

Am I locked in?

FOURTEEN

Alexia pounded on the solid oak door, yelling, "Help! I'm locked in."

Her parents' bedroom was at the other end of the hallway, but if her father was in there, he should hear her.

After five minutes, she halted, gasping for a deep breath of air. Her heartbeat raced, and her fists ached.

She whirled around and scanned the room for anything she could use to force the door to open. Her gaze fixed on the landline phone on her desk, and she hastened to it. When she picked up the receiver, she waited for the dial tone to punch in the first number. There was no sound. She pushed the talk button but still nothing.

It didn't work.

This had to be the work of the saboteur. Had he cut the line?

She stepped to the window nearby and opened the curtains. She already knew her second floor bedroom window wouldn't be a way out because of the eighteen-foot drop into the garden below with huge ornamental rocks littered throughout it.

This was when she wished she didn't have a lock both on the inside and outside of her room. She sank into the desk chair, and the implications of her being locked in her room really sank in. He was in the house!

Again, her attention riveted on the door. Maybe she could pick the lock. With what? It wasn't like she'd ever done that. Then she noticed the hinges on the door. What if she could work the pins out of them? She could get out that way.

With her hope renewed, she searched for something to use. It needed to be strong enough to pry and drive the pin out.

A flathead screwdriver might work, but she didn't have one.

Then she remembered drinking tea in her room earlier and using a spoon to stir in honey. She shifted to look behind her on the desk. Her cup was still there and the spoon beside it. She snatched it up and hurried to the door. As she worked on the middle hinge, putting all her strength into it, sweat beaded her brow and rolled into her eyes.

She worked the top of the pin moving it up—barely. Then she jammed the end of the spoon handle in the bottom hole and tried to shove the pin further up. Again, it barely moved, and she wasn't even positive about that. While struggling to loosen the hinge, she shouted, "Help!" just in case someone was in the house and could hear her that wasn't the saboteur.

Questions flooded her mind. Was he still here? Why and how did he lock her in the room? Where did he get the key? There was a skeleton key in the kitchen and upstairs in a hallway table. Where are *her parents and Uncle Hank?* Is her dad still in his bedroom?

She was afraid of the answers. Instead, she poured everything she had into dislodging the middle hinge. Then she would work on the lower one. After that she might be able to wrench the door loose and not have to work on the top one.

As she dragged calming breaths into her lungs, the scent of smoke invaded her room. She dropped to her knees, bent over and pressed her cheek against the carpet to smell the air drifting in from the hallway.

Definitely smoke!

* * *

Cole pushed the speed past the legal limit. He had to get back to the ranch. The landlines were down, and no one answered the cell phones he'd called: Alexia's, Red's, Hank's, and Charlie's. Before he drove into the dead zone, he'd called Sheriff Anderson, and he would send the nearest deputy to check on what was happening. Cole tried to feel a little better knowing that the sheriff would also go to the Flying Red, but his gut churned with apprehension.

Something was going down, and he was miles away. He couldn't let Alexia down again.

He floored the accelerator.

When he was about ten miles away, he spotted a plume of smoke roiling upward and spreading out from the approximate location of the ranch.

Please, Lord, protect Alexia and the others. I love her. I can't lose her again.

Please help Alexia to handle the fire.

After having a close call in a fire and their son dying, she had to be freaking out.

The closer he came to the Flying Red, he could tell something big was burning in the part of the ranch where the main house and barn were.

At the opened gate, he slowed enough to make the turn then pressed the accelerator again. His gaze riveted on the house, smoke billowing from it.

He hoped everyone was out by now.

Ranch hands raced with buckets and hoses toward the house. No fire truck from town yet, but the sheriff was outside, trying to organize the employees to fight the fire.

Cole slammed to a stop, the truck's rear end fishtailing.

The fire seemed to be contained at the moment to the first floor, where the family usually would be at this time. Where were they? Still inside? This had to be set deliberately.

By someone who knew Alexia's past. Marcie? She'd worked for the family since Alexia came back to Montana, so she could know about the fire in Georgia. She had ties to Rusty. Maybe Alexia was the target all along—not Red or the company. That thought chilled him.

But why would Marcie come after them? Did she know something about the long-ago relationship between Red and her mother?

Cole shouldered the car door open and rushed to the sheriff. Cole still didn't see Alexia, Red, Helen, Hank, or Charlie.

Cole planted himself in front of Sheriff Anderson. "Where's the family?"

"My deputy and Keith are trying to get inside. The fire seems to be everywhere and the doors won't budge."

Cole started for the porch, shouting over his shoulder, "Where's Marcie?"

"I don't know. Charlie and a deputy went looking for her" The sheriff dispatched the last cowhand and hurried after Cole. "The fire department should be here any minute."

At the rate the fire was spreading, Cole didn't know if their presence would make a difference.

* * *

Exhausted, Alexia finally worked the bottom hinge free. The smoke leaking under the door was getting thicker. Her hands and arms throbbed with the exertion. She couldn't even afford a moment to rest. She prayed she could pry the door loose enough that she could get out of the room.

She pulled the bottom of the door with what strength she had left, hoping it would wrench the top hinge loose. The bigger the space along the side grew, the more smoke poured into the room. She ran into her bathroom, grabbed a towel and doused it with water. As she rushed back, she wrapped the wet terry cloth around her neck and face, covering her mouth and nose.

She continued to force the door from its frame. If she'd been locked into her room, maybe her dad was, too, even though she hadn't heard him yell. Over her thundering heartbeat resonating through her head, sirens sounded, fueling her to keep going. Help was on the way. But the urgency didn't quieten with that thought. She knew firsthand how quickly a fire could spread.

Finally, the wooden frame gave, and with one last yank on the door, it swung open from the bottom enough that she could get out. She squeezed through the gap into a smoke-filled hallway. With smoke less dense near the floor, she crawled toward her father's bedroom. When she passed the staircase, she slowed her pace for a few seconds to see if she could use it to get to the first floor. Coughs racked her. Yellow-orange flames ate their way up the steps, cutting off any avenue of escape. She came to a stop and stared at the blaze devouring the stairs. The sight paralyzed her.

Just like three years ago. But this time she was trapped on the other side.

Move! It's not too late.

The wet towel began to slip from her face. Its movement jerked her back to the here and now.

I can't give up.

She continued to the other end of the corridor, coughing. Her eyes stung, making seeing even more difficult. Sweat rolled down her face from the heat. She would think of another way out of the house once she found her father.

When she reached her parents' room, she rose and tried to open the door. Locked like hers.

The crackling of the fire filled her mind. Boom! She pivoted, seeing the glow of the flames through the thickening smoke.

Think!

Her gaze latched onto a long table across from her father's room. She jerked the drawer out and searched for the skeleton key kept there in case of emergencies. Her fingers latched onto it, and she rushed back across the hall, inserted the key in the lock, and opened the door.

Through the veil of smoke, she spied her dad on the bed, not moving, his eyes closed.

Another heart attack?

* * *

The fire spread from the foyer at the front of the house into the middle of the house. Cole couldn't wait for the fire department, nor try to contain a blaze that was rapidly growing out of control. He had to act fast. He needed to find a way inside. He ran toward the back. The kitchen was on the right side at the rear. As he used his key and let himself inside, Keith and Charlie followed.

"Who's in here?" Charlie asked.

"Alexia, Red, Hank, and Helen. They could be in the house office or..." There were a lot of possibilities with four missing and a large house. "Did you find Marcie at the ranch?"

"No. The deputy's still looking, but her car's gone. She was here earlier. The deputy said something about her knowing the Moose Creek shooter. Do you think she's behind this?"

"It's looking like that." Cole grabbed dishtowels for each of them to cover their faces and rounded the island to wet them. He nearly tripped over Alexia's mom lying on the floor. He knelt and felt her pulse. "Helen's here and alive. Charlie get her outside. Keith and I will look for the others."

While Charlie scooped up Helen, Cole headed into the rear hallway. The office was on the left side at the back of the house. Through the dense smoke, Cole hunkered low and felt his way using the wall as his guide. The office door was shut—and locked. He and Keith took turns kicking the door right below the knob. It burst open on the fifth attempt. Cole rushed inside, praying the others were in the room and alive. But all he saw was Hank slumped over, his head resting on top of papers on a table.

Keith made his way to Hank. "I'll take care of him. See if you can find Alexia and Red." He checked Hank's pulse and added, "He's alive."

Cole hurried out into the hall, checking the nearby rooms as he retraced his steps to the center of the house and the corridor that led to the front. Alexia was going to take a nap. Was she still asleep? Was she upstairs?

Boom!

A crash filled the air, coming from the foyer. His lungs burned with each breath he took in as he drew closer to the entryway. Through the thick haze, he saw a wall of heat and flames roiling toward him.

Blocking him from going any further.

Is this how Alexia felt when their home burned down?

Helpless.

Losing hope.

Alone.

Keeping an eye on any break in the fire,

he backed away, curling his hands into fists at his side. The blaze was between him and the staircase.

Someone clasped his shoulder from behind.

$$* * *$$

"Dad, wake up!" Alexia shook him.

He moaned.

"The house is on fire. Get up!" She jostled him again.

His eyelids fluttered open. He blinked. "What?"

"There's a fire." She tugged on his arm. "We need to get out of here."

Sluggish, he struggled to sit up. Coughs overtook him. He hunched over. "What's..." Another round of hacking shook his body.

She wrapped her towel around his lower face then pulled him toward the edge of the bed. "We can't go down the stairs, but I have a way out of here."

He looked at her as though he didn't understand what she was saying, but as she drew him toward the hallway, he didn't resist. Had they been drugged? When? How?

The bedroom next to his was above the kitchen where the roof of the outside patio met the house. Urging him to move faster, she practically dragged him across the room to the window overlooking the backyard.

"We're going to climb outside here and yell for help." She raised the window. "I heard the sirens. The fire department should be here by now. Dad," she said in a loud voice and waited for his full attention, "I'm going first. Then I'll help you out the window. Do you understand?"

Dazed-looking, he nodded slowly.

Alexia climbed out onto the sloping roof of the patio, planting her feet apart to stabilize herself as she assisted her father. He crawled out of the window, holding tight to her. She didn't know if he was alert enough to walk to the edge without falling.

"Dad, sit. We're going to scooch to the side."

When her father didn't protest the suggestion, she realized somehow they had to be drugged earlier. He wasn't acting right at all.

As she neared the ledge, she shouted, "Help," over and over.

Charlie, carrying her mother, came out from under the roof of the patio and looked up. "Someone will be right back with a ladder."

"Is Mom—" Her throat tightened around the word okay.

"She's alive. Cole and Keith are looking for Hank and you two in the house," Charlie said over his shoulder as he continued toward the front.

A minute later, two firefighters, carrying a ladder, jogged toward them.

"Dad, we'll be all right." But would Cole and the others make it outside safely?

* * *

Cole tensed and spun around, shrugging off the hand on his shoulder. Through the smoke, like a heavy fog, a firefighter stood a few feet away. While the heat of the blaze grew warmer on Cole's back, the popping, sizzling, and crackling of the fire grew louder—nearer.

Before Cole could say anything, the man shouted, "You've got to get out of here."

"I'm still looking for Red and Alexia."

"They're outside. Everyone's out. I told Alexia I'd find you and let you know." The firefighter motioned for Cole to go first.

They're alive. Relief surged through him until he heard a crash right behind him.

"Go!" The man shouted through his mask.

As Cole raced down the hallway with the firefighter following him, the ceiling behind him fell to the first floor, shaking the house. Trying to hold his breath, he increased his speed, thankful that he knew his way around the place since he couldn't see more than a foot in front of him. He felt a long rumble as if Alexia's home was folding in on itself. He burst into the kitchen, threw a glance over his shoulder at the firefighter, and kept going until he was out on the patio.

Although smoke laced the outside air,

Cole took in several deep breaths for his oxygen-depleted lungs while continuing to move away from the blaze. A series of coughing spells one after another, racked his body.

"You need to see the paramedics." The firefighter who'd come in to get him clasped his arm and steered him around the side of the house and to the nearest ambulance.

The EMT immediately put an oxygen mask over Cole's head and directed him to sit in the back of the emergency vehicle while the other paramedic treated Hank, who lay on the gurney in the rear.

Cole sat on the bumper. Until he did, he didn't realize how exhausted he was. Even though the firefighter had told him Alexia was all right, Cole had to see for himself. He looked around for her.

She was in the second ambulance about five yards away with a mask over her face. Her dad and mom were sitting next to her, doing the same. Alexia swiveled around, and their gazes embraced across the distance.

He loved her. He wasn't going anywhere. This was home to him.

Marcie didn't win. Everyone got out safely, and the house could be rebuilt.

But had Sheriff Anderson found Marcie? Or had she gotten away, so she could continue her reign of terror?

FIFTEEN

While Marcie was escorted into the sheriff's interview room, Cole stood leaning against the wall while Red sat at the table. The deputy seated Marcie, who they had found out was Red's daughter, across from him and handcuffed her hands to a bar in front of her. Then he left them alone.

Marcie had come to the kitchen the day of the fire to return the plate of cookies Helen had baked for her. Alexia's mom had felt bad that she had been sick most likely because someone was after the family. While Helen went into the pantry, Marcie doctored the coffee with a strong sleeping aid and then acted as if she'd left out the back door. She said good-bye, opened, then closed the back door without going outside. She left the kitchen and hid in the house until the time was right to start the fire.

"Why didn't you let me know who you were?" Red asked Marcie. "Why did you do all those awful things?"

For a long moment, all she did was drill a glare into Red.

"You discarded my mother. I wasn't going to let you do the same to me," she finally answered, her hands balled so tightly Cole could see her white knuckles.

"No, I wouldn't have. I never knew Marilyn was even pregnant."

Marcie blinked rapidly and dropped her head. "I don't believe you." She raised her chin and narrowed her gaze on Red. "That's not what she said. She told me you were the reason her life ended up like it did. She never wanted me and neither did you. I saw how you doted on your daughter. When Mom died, I decided to make you pay for our misery." Marcie jumped to her feet and tried to lunge across the table at Red. "I hate you!"

A pallor to his face, Red shoved his chair back and rose. "I took you under my wing. I taught you trick riding and highlighted your act."

"You never asked about my past."

"Would you have told me if I had?"

She smiled, no humor in her expression. "You'll never know. I don't want to talk to you ever again."

"Let me at least pay for a lawyer rather than have a court appointed one."

Her gaze stabbed through him. "I don't want your money now. Too late." She lowered her head and stared at her handcuffed wrists.

Cole approached a stunned Red. "Let's go. There's no reason to stay."

Red let Cole guide him from the interview room. As though on automatic mode, Red thanked Sheriff Anderson and then walked to the front door.

When Cole settled behind the steering wheel, he remained quiet until they left the town. "I'm sorry, Red. From all I learned about her in Blue Sky, she wasn't a good daughter to Marilyn either."

"Will I ever be able to move beyond the mistake I made twenty-four years ago?"

"I know that Alexia and Helen have forgiven you. You just have to forgive yourself. Ask yourself what you would have done if you'd known about Marcie from the beginning."

Silence ruled for the next ten minutes before Red sighed. "Helen knew about my affair with Marilyn. Helen would have accepted Marcie into our lives because she's the type of woman who doesn't want to go to bed with anger in her heart. I would have wanted a say in raising Marcie."

"Then you have your answer. You would have done the right thing by Marcie if you'd been given the chance."

"Marcie might not want anything from me now, but she's gonna have my prayers."

As Cole neared the Flying Red Ranch, he was determined to put his own life back together.

* * *

Staying in the first house built on the ranch by her grandparents, Alexia paced from one end of the living room to the other.

"Honey, you should sit and rest. This past week with the fire and dealing with the aftermath has taken its toll whether you want to admit it or not. Besides, the pacing won't bring your father and Cole home any sooner." Mom looked up from her knitting.

"I should have gone rather than Dad."

"Red needed to deal with this. I'm just glad he let Cole go with him."

Finally, Alexia took a chair across from her mother on the couch. "After all that's happened, how can you calmly sit there and knit a scarf?"

Mom raised one of her eyebrows. "You think I'm calm?" She shook her head. "I knit when I'm nervous and need to do something with my hands or to do something mindless so I don't think about what I really should be thinking of."

"You're upset at Dad? I thought you two had worked things out years ago."

"No, I'm not. Red and I have worked through what happened back then. I forgave him long ago, and his daughter's attempts to kill us haven't changed that. But I see how upset he is. He didn't know he had another child. Marilyn never told him. He regrets all those years he could have been involved in Marcie's life, maybe prevented her anger. He blames this whole thing on himself."

"I have a half-sister, and she tried to kill me. All I can say is I'm glad that Sheriff Anderson has her locked up in jail. These past weeks have been awful."

"But something good came out of all of this. We need to concentrate on that."

Alexia stared at her mom as though she'd lost it. "What good? You lost your home. People were hurt, almost killed. I worry that Dad will have another heart attack from all the stress."

"Cole is back in your life. Don't tell me you don't love him. I can see it on your face every time he's in the room. And he feels the same way. You two need to talk. Things should settle down now that Marcie was captured in Billings. There's no more threat to us. The house will be rebuilt but not by Red and me."

Alexia sat forward. "Who?"

"You and Cole. This home is perfect for your dad and me."

"Mom, Cole and I have forgiven each other over what happened three years ago, but we haven't talked about getting married again." She hoped they would, but she didn't know how he felt.

"You will. I know it in here." Her mother patted her chest over her heart. "I hope you can let go of your anger toward Marcie. It'll only hurt you in the end."

Alexia thought about how her mother dealt with being upset at a person. Through the years, she'd worked to put the problem and wrath behind her—as the Lord wanted. Mom was right. Marcie would win if Alexia didn't. If only Marilyn had let Dad know about Marcie. Then Alexia could have had the sister she'd always wanted. "Mom, I'll eventually forgive her. Cole and I have each other, and it does feel so much better than being angry all the time."

Helen smiled. "Why don't you tell me who called a while back? I gathered it had to do with our company."

Alexia relaxed back and grinned. "I was confirming the first place we'll be holding our rodeo camp. Not only do they want us to hold it the day before the rodeo, but they also want the camp participants to be part of the opening ceremony. They loved the idea, and they're going to start advertising immediately. And although we aren't doing the Fourth of July celebration in Billings, I proposed doing a camp for a day as part of their big celebration. The manager liked the idea and will get back to me soon about it."

"The best part is it's going to be yours to run. I won't have to brow beat your dad into taking it easy."

Alexia chuckled. When her dad told her yesterday she would be traveling more, at first, she didn't realize he'd meant he was putting her totally in charge of the rodeo camp part of the company. When she'd figured it out, she knew their relationship would only be strengthened over time. The past week had been a time to bond as they hadn't in a very long time.

The crunching sound of the road gravel out front alerted Alexia a vehicle was approaching. She glanced out the picture window.

Cole pulled up in his truck. He'd driven her father into town because Marcie had agreed to see him. Dad had needed that.

"How's your dad look?" her mother asked from behind Alexia.

"At peace." She rose and headed for the front door.

* * *

Later that night, Alexia stood outside on the front porch, staring at the sunset, streaks of pink, orange, and yellow painting the sky in brilliance. She loved this time a day as the animals settled down and nature grew quiet.

The sound of the door behind her opening and closing alerted her to Cole's presence. Her heart rate picked up speed. She gripped the railing, anticipating his touch, and wasn't disappointed when he clasped her shoulders and drew her back against him.

He leaned close to her ear and whispered, "Your dad just asked me to stay and help you run the company. He wants to slow down and spend more time with Helen."

Alexia smiled. "And what did you tell him?"

"That the decision was yours to make. The only way I would stay is if you and I remarried." Cole released his hold on her shoulders and turned her to face him. "I love you, and I couldn't be near you without wanting you every day."

Tingles raced up and down her body. "I wouldn't want you to be here unless you're my husband. I can't be near you and not want you every day either." She entwined her fingers together behind his neck and tugged him close until her mouth touched his.

He took over and deepened the kiss as though they hadn't kissed in years. She pressed herself flat against him. All her love flowed into the physical connection. He nibbled a path to her earlobe and took it gently between his teeth.

"Then I'll accept the job," he whispered against her skin, chilling her in a delicious way.

"I love you, and I think we should marry right away. I've missed you."

He lifted her up onto the railing and held her against him. "You won't get an argument from me. Tomorrow isn't soon enough."

Again, he claimed her mouth—and her heart.

DEADLY HUNT

Book 1 in
Strong Women, Extraordinary Situations
by Margaret Daley

All bodyguard Tess Miller wants is a vacation. But when a wounded stranger stumbles into her isolated cabin in the Arizona mountains, Tess becomes his lifeline. When Shane Burkhart opens his eyes, all he can focus on is his guardian angel leaning over him. And in the days to come he will need a guardian angel while being hunted by someone who wants him dead.

DEADLY INTENT

Book 2 in
Strong Women, Extraordinary Situations
by Margaret Daley

Texas Ranger Sarah Osborn thought she would never see her high school sweetheart, Ian O'Leary, again. But fifteen years later, Ian, an ex-FBI agent, has someone targeting him, and she's assigned to the case. Can Sarah protect Ian and her heart?

DEADLY HOLIDAY

Book 3 in
Strong Women, Extraordinary Situations
by Margaret Daley

Tory Caldwell witnesses a hit-and-run, but when the dead victim disappears from the scene, police doubt a crime has been committed. Tory is threatened when she keeps insisting she saw a man killed and the only one who believes her is her neighbor, Jordan Steele. Together, can they solve the mystery of the disappearing body and stay alive?

DEADLY COUNTDOWN

Book Four in
Strong Women, Extraordinary Situations
by Margaret Daley

Allie Martin, a widow, has a secret protector who manipulates her life without anyone knowing until...

When Remy Broussard, an injured police officer, returns to Port David, Louisiana to visit before his medical leave is over, he discovers his childhood friend, Allie Martin, is being stalked. As Remy protects Allie and tries to find her stalker, they realize their feelings go beyond friendship.

When the stalker is found, they begin to explore the deeper feelings they have for each other, only to have a more sinister threat come between them. Will Allie be able to save Remy before he dies at the hand of a maniac?

DEADLY NOEL

Book Five in
Strong Women, Extraordinary Situations
by Margaret Daley

Assistant DA, Kira Davis, convicted the wrong man—Gabriel Michaels, a single dad with a young daughter. When new evidence was brought forth, his conviction was overturned, and Gabriel returned home to his ranch to put his life back together. Although Gabriel is free, the murderer of his wife is still out there and resumes killing women. In a desperate alliance, Kira and Gabriel join forces to find the true identity of the person terrorizing their town. Will they be able to forgive the past and find the killer before it's too late?

DEADLY DOSE

Book Six in
Strong Women, Extraordinary Situations
by Margaret Daley

Drugs. Murder. Redemption.

When Jessie Michaels discovers a letter written to her by her deceased best friend, she is determined to find who murdered Mary Lou, at first thought to be a victim of a serial killer by the police. Jessie's questions lead to an attempt on her life. The last man she wanted to come to her aid was Josh Morgan, who had been instrumental in her brother going to prison. Together they uncover a drug ring that puts them both in danger. Will Jessie and Josh find the killer? Love? Or will one of them fall victim to a DEADLY DOSE?

DEADLY LEGACY

Book Seven in
Strong Women, Extraordinary Situations
by Margaret Daley

Down on her luck, single mom, Lacey St. John, believes her life has finally changed for the better when she receives an inheritance from a wealthy stranger. Her ancestral home she'd thought forever lost has been transformed into a lucrative bed and breakfast guaranteed to bring much-needed financial security. Her happiness is complete until strange happenings erode her sense of well being. When her life is threatened, she turns to neighbor, Sheriff Ryan McNeil, for help. He promises to solve the mystery of who's ruining her newfound peace of mind, but when her troubles escalate to the point that her every move leads to danger, she's unsure who to trust. Is the strong, capable neighbor she's falling for as amazing as he seems? Or could he be the man who wants her dead?

DEADLY NIGHT, SILENT NIGHT

Book Eight in
Strong Women, Extraordinary Situations
by Margaret Daley

Revenge. Sabotage. Second Chances.

Widow Rebecca Howard runs a successful store chain that is being targeted during the holiday season. Detective Alex Kincaid, best friends with Rebecca's twin brother, is investigating the hacking of the store's computer system. When the attacks become personal, Alex must find the assailant before Rebecca, the woman he's falling in love with, is murdered.

Excerpt from DEADLY HUNT
Strong Women, Extraordinary Situations
Book One

ONE

Tess Miller pivoted as something thumped against the door. An animal? With the cabin's isolation in the Arizona mountains, she couldn't take any chances. She crossed the distance to a combination-locked cabinet and quickly entered the numbers. After withdrawing the shotgun, she checked to make sure it was loaded then started toward the door to bolt it, adrenaline pumping through her veins.

Silence. Had she imagined the noise? Maybe her work was getting to her, making her paranoid. But as she crept toward the entrance, a faint scratching against the wood told her otherwise. Her senses sharpened like they would at work. Only this time, there was no client to protect. Just her own skin. Her heartbeat accelerated as she planted herself firmly. She reached toward the handle to throw the bolt.

The door crashed open before she touched the knob. She scrambled backwards and to the side at the same time steadying the weapon in her grasp. A large man tumbled into the cabin, collapsing face down at her feet. His head rolled to the side. His eyelids fluttered, then closed.

Stunned, Tess froze. She stared at the man's profile.

Who is he?

The stranger moaned. She knelt next to him to assess what was wrong. Her gaze traveled down his long length. Clotted blood matted his unruly black hair. A plaid flannel shirt, torn in a couple of places, exposed scratches and minor cuts. A rag that had been tied around his leg was soaked with blood. Laying her weapon at her side, she eased the piece of cloth down an inch and discovered a hole in his thigh, still bleeding.

He's been shot.

Is he alone? She bolted to her feet. Sidestepping his prone body, she snatched up the shotgun again and surveyed the area outside her cabin. All she saw was the sparse, lonely terrain. With little vegetation, hiding places were limited in the immediate vicinity, and she had no time to check further away. She examined the ground to see which direction he'd come from. There weren't any visible red splotches and only one set of large footprints coming from around the side of the cabin. His fall must have started his bleeding again.

Another groan pierced the early morning quiet. She returned to the man, knelt, and pressed her two fingers into the side of his neck. His pulse was rapid, thready, and his skin was cold with a slight bluish tint.

He was going into shock. Her emergency-care training took over. She jumped to her feet, grabbed her backpack off the wooden table and found her first aid kit. After securing a knife from the shelf next to the fireplace, she hurried back to the man and moved his legs slightly so she could close the door and lock it. She yanked her sleeping bag off the bunk, spread it open, then rolled the stranger onto it. When she'd maneuvered his body face-up, she covered his torso.

For a few seconds she stared at him. He had a day's growth of beard covering his jaw. Was he running away from someone— the law? What happened to him? From his disheveled look, he'd been out in the elements all night. She patted him down for a wallet but found no identification. Her suspicion skyrocketed.

Her attention fixed again on the side of his head where blood had coagulated. The wound wasn't bleeding anymore. She would tend that injury later.

As her gaze quickly trekked toward his left leg, her mind registered his features—a strong, square jaw, a cleft in his chin, long, dark eyelashes that fanned the top of his cheeks in stark contrast to the pallor that tinged his tanned skin. Her attention focused on the blood-soaked cloth that had been used to stop the bleeding.

Tess snatched a pair of latex gloves from her first aid kit, then snapped them on and untied the cloth, removing it from his leg. There was a small bullet hole in the front part of his thigh. Was that an exit wound? She prayed it was and checked the back of his leg. She found a larger wound there, which meant the bullet had exited from the front.

Shot from behind. Was he ambushed? A shiver snaked down her spine.

At least she didn't have to deal with extracting a bullet. What she did have to cope with was bad enough. The very seclusion she'd craved this past week was her enemy now. The closest road was nearly a day's hike away.

First, stop the bleeding. Trying not to jostle him too much, she cut his left jean leg away to expose the injury more clearly.

She scanned the cabin for something to elevate his lower limbs. A footstool. She used that to raise his legs higher than his heart. Then she put pressure on his wounds to stop the renewed flow of blood from the bullet holes. She cleansed the areas, then bandaged them. After that, she cleaned the injury on his head and covered it with a gauze pad.

When she finished, she sat back and waited to see if indeed the bleeding from the two wounds in his thigh had stopped. From where the holes were, it looked as though the bullet had passed through muscles, missing bone and major blood vessels. But from the condition the man had been in when he'd arrived, he was lucky he'd survived this long. If the bullet had hit an inch over, he would have bled out.

She looked at his face again. "What happened to you?"

Even in his unconscious, unkempt state, his features gave an impression of authority and quiet power. In her line of work, she'd learned to think the worst and question everything. Was he a victim? Was there somebody else out there who'd been injured? Who had pulled the trigger—a criminal or the law?

Then it hit her. She was this man's lifeline. If she hadn't been here in this cabin at this time, he would have surely died in these mountains. Civilization was a ten-hour hike from here. From his appearance, he'd already pushed himself beyond most men's endurance.

Lord, I need Your help. I've been responsible for people's lives before, but this is different. I'm alone up here, except for You.

Her memories of her last assignment inundated Tess. Guarding an eight-year-old girl whose rich parents had received threats had mentally exhausted her. The child had nearly been kidnapped and so frightened when Tess had gone to protect her. It had been the longest month of her life, praying every day that nothing happened to Clare. By the end Tess had hated leaving the girl whose parents were usually too busy for her. This vacation had been paramount to her.

The stranger moaned. His eyelids

fluttered, and his uninjured leg moved a few inches.

"Oh, no you don't. Stay still. I just got you stabilized." She anchored his shoulders to the floor and prayed even more. Even if he were a criminal, she wouldn't let him die.

Slowly the stranger's restlessness abated. Tess exhaled a deep, steadying breath through pursed lips, examining the white bandage for any sign of red. None. She sighed again.

When she'd done all she could, she covered him completely with a blanket and then made her way to the fireplace. The last log burned in the middle of a pile of ashes. Though the days were still warm in October, the temperature would drop into the forties come evening. She'd need more fuel.

Tess crossed the few steps to the kitchen, lifted the coffeepot and poured the last of it into her mug. Her hands shook as she lifted the drink to her lips. She dealt in life and death situations in her work as a bodyguard all the time, but this was different. How often did half-dead bodies crash through her front door? Worse than that, she was all alone up here. This man's survival depended on her. She was accustomed to protecting people, not doctoring them. The coffee in her stomach mixed with a healthy dose of fear, and she swallowed the sudden nausea.

Turning back, she studied the stranger.

Maybe it was a hunting accident. If so, why didn't he have identification on him? Where were the other hunters? How did he get shot? All over again, the questions flooded her mind with a pounding intensity, her natural curiosity not appeased.

The crude cabin, with its worn, wooden floor and its walls made of rough old logs, was suddenly no longer the retreat she'd been anticipating for months. Now it was a cage, trapping her here with a man who might not live.

No, he had to. She would make sure of it—somehow.

* * *

Through a haze Shane Burkhart saw a beautiful vision bending over him with concern clouding her face. Had he died? No, he hurt too much to be dead. Every muscle in his body ached. A razor-sharp pain spread throughout him until it consumed his sanity. It emanated from his leg and vied with the pounding in his head.

He tried to swallow, but his mouth and throat felt as if a soiled rag had been stuffed down there. He tasted dirt and dust. Forcing his eyelids to remain open, he licked his dry lips and whispered, "Water."

The woman stood and moved away from him. Where was he? He remembered ... Every effort—even to think—zapped what little energy he had.

He needed to ask something. What? His mind blanked as pain drove him toward a dark void.

* * *

Tess knelt next to the stranger with the cup of water on the floor beside her, disappointed she couldn't get some answers to her myriad questions. With her muscles stiff from sitting on the hard floor for so long, she rose and stretched. She would chop some much-needed wood for a fire later, and then she'd scout the terrain near the cabin to check for signs of others. She couldn't shake the feeling there might be others—criminals—nearby who were connected to the stranger.

She bent over and grazed the back of her hand across his forehead to make sure her patient wasn't feverish, combing away a lock of black hair. Neither she nor he needed that complication in these primitive conditions. The wounds were clean. The rest was in the Lord's hands.

After slipping on a light jacket, she grabbed her binoculars and shotgun, stuffed her handgun into her waistband and went outside, relishing the cool breeze that whipped her long hair around her shoulders.

She strode toward the cliff nearby and surveyed the area, taking in the rugged landscape, the granite spirals jutting up from the tan and moss green of the valley below. The path to the cabin was visible part of the way up the mountain, and she couldn't see any evidence of hunters or hikers. Close to the bottom a grove of sycamores and oaks, their leaves shades of green, yellow and brown, obstructed her view. But again, aside from a circling falcon, there was no movement. She watched the bird swoop into the valley and snatch something from the ground. She shuddered, knowing something had just become dinner.

Her uncle, who owned the cabin, had told her he'd chopped down a tree and hauled it to the summit, so there would be wood for her. Now, all she had to do was split some of the logs, a job she usually enjoyed.

Today, she didn't want to be gone long in case something happened to the stranger. She located the medium-size tree trunk, checked on her patient to make sure he was still sleeping and set about chopping enough wood for the evening and night. The temperature could plummet in this mountainous desert terrain.

The repetitive sound of the axe striking the wood lured Tess into a hypnotic state until a yelp pierced her mind. She dropped the axe and hurried toward the cabin. Shoving the door open wide, she crossed the threshold to find the stranger trying to rise from the sleeping bag. Pain carved lines deeper into his grimacing face. His groan propelled her forward.

"Leaving so soon." Her lighthearted tone didn't reflect the anxiety she felt at his condition. "You just got here." She knelt beside him, breathing in the antiseptic scent that tangled with the musky odor of the room.

Propping his body up with his elbows, he stared at her, trying to mask the effort that little movement had cost him. "Where ... am ... I?" His speech slow, he shifted, struggling to make himself more comfortable.

"You don't remember how you got here?" Tess placed her arm behind his back to support him.

"No."

"What happened to you?"

The man sagged wearily against her. "Water."

His nearness jolted her senses, as though she were the one who had been deprived of water and overwhelmed with thirst. She glanced over her shoulder to where she'd placed the tin cup. After lowering him onto the sleeping bag, she quickly retrieved the drink and helped him take a couple of sips.

"Why do I ... hurt?" he murmured, his eyelids fluttering.

He didn't remember what happened to him. Head wounds could lead to memory loss, but was it really that? Her suspicion continued to climb. "You were shot in the leg," she said, her gaze lifting to assess his reaction.

A blank stare looked back at her. "What?" He blinked, his eyelids sliding down.

"You were shot. Who are you? What happened?"

She waited for a moment, but when he didn't reply, she realized he'd drifted off to sleep. Or maybe he was faking it. Either way, he was only prolonging the moment when he would have to face her with answers to her questions. The mantle of tension she wore when she worked a job fell over her shoulders, and all the stress she'd shed the day before when she'd arrived at the cabin late in the afternoon returned and multiplied.

Rising, she dusted off the knees of her jeans, her attention fixed on his face. Some color tinted his features now, although they still remained pale beneath his bronzed skin. Noting his even breathing, she left the cabin and walked around studying the area before returning to chop the wood. She completed her task in less than an hour with enough logs to last a few days.

With her arms full of the fuel, she kicked the ajar door open wider and reentered the one-room, rustic abode. She found the stranger awake, more alert. He hadn't moved an inch.

"It's good to see you're up." She crossed to the fireplace and stacked the wood.

"I thought I might have imagined you."

"Nope." As she swept toward him, she smiled. "Before you decide to take another nap, what is your name?"

"Shane Burkhart, and you?"

"Tess Miller."

"Water please?"

"Sure." She hurried to him with the tin cup and lifted him a few inches from the floor.

"Where am I?"

"A nine to ten hour walk from any kind of help, depending on how fast you hike. That's what I've always loved about this place, its isolation. But right now I'd trade it for a phone or a neighbor with a medical degree."

"You're all I have?"

"At the moment."

Those words came out in a whisper as the air between them thickened, cementing a bond that Tess wanted to deny, to break. But she was his lifeline. And this was different from her job as a bodyguard. Maybe because he had invaded her personal alone time—time she needed to refill her well to allow her to do her best work.

She couldn't shake that feeling that perhaps it was something else.

"What happened to you?"

His forehead wrinkled in thought, his expression shadowed. "You said I was shot?"

"Yes. How? Who shot you?"

"I don't remember." He rubbed his temple. "All I remember is ... standing on a cliff." Frustration infused each word.

Okay, this wasn't going to be easy. Usually it wasn't. If she thought of him as an innocent, then hounding him for answers would only add to his confusion, making getting those answers harder.

She rose and peered toward the fireplace. "I thought about fixing some soup for lunch." Normally she wouldn't have chosen soup, but she didn't think he'd be able to eat much else and he needed his strength. "You should try,"—she returned her gaze to him and noticed his eyes were closed—"to eat."

He didn't respond. Leaning over him, she gently shook his arm. His face twitched, but he didn't open his eyes.

Restless, she made her way outside with her shotgun and binoculars, leaving the door open in case he needed her. She scoured anyplace within a hundred yards that could be a hiding place but found nothing. Then she perched on a crop of rocks that projected out from the cliff, giving her a majestic vista of the mountain range and ravines. Autumn crept over the landscape, adding touches of yellows, oranges and reds to her view. Twice a year she visited this cabin, and this was always her favorite spot.

With her binoculars, she studied the landscape around her. Still no sight of anyone else. All the questions she had concerning Shane Burkhart—if that was his name—continued to plague her. Until she got some answers, she'd keep watch on him and the area. She'd learned in her work that she needed to plan for trouble, so if it came she'd be ready. If it didn't, that was great. Often, however, it did. And a niggling sensation along her spine told her something was definitely wrong.

Although there were hunters in the fall in these mountains, she had a strong suspicion that Shane's wound was no accident. The feeling someone shot him deliberately took hold and grew, reinforcing her plan to be extra vigilant.

* * *

Mid-afternoon, when the sun was its strongest, Tess stood on her perch and worked the kinks out of her body. Her stranger needed sleep, but she needed to check on him every hour to make sure everything was all right. After one last scan of the terrain, she headed to the door. Inside, her gaze immediately flew to Shane who lay on the floor nearby.

He stared up at her, a smile fighting its way past the pain reflected in his eyes. "I thought you'd deserted me."

"How long have you been awake?"

"Not long."

"I'll make us some soup." Although the desire to have answers was still strong, she'd forgotten to eat anything today except the energy bar she'd had before he'd arrived. But now her stomach grumbled with hunger.

He reached out for the tin cup a few feet from him. She quickly grabbed it and gave him a drink, this time placing it on the floor beside him.

"I have acetaminophen if you want some for the pain," she said as she straightened, noting the shadows in his eyes. "I imagine your leg and head are killing you."

"Don't use that word. I don't want to think about how close I came to dying. If it hadn't been for you ..."

Again that connection sprang up between them, and she wanted to deny it. She didn't want to be responsible for anyone in her personal life. She had enough of that in her professional life. Her trips to the cabin were the only time she was able to let go of the stress and tension that were so much a part of her life. She stifled a sigh. It wasn't like he'd asked to be shot. "Do you want some acetaminophen?"

"Acetaminophen? That's like throwing a glass of water on a forest fire." He cocked a grin that fell almost instantly. "But I guess I should try."

"Good."

She delved into her first aid kit and produced the bottle of painkillers. After shaking a few into her palm, she gave them to him and again helped him to sip some water. The continual close contact with him played havoc with her senses. Usually she managed to keep her distance—at least emotionally—from her clients and others, but this whole situation was forcing her out of her comfort zone and much closer to him than she was used to.

After he swallowed the pills, she stood and stepped back. "I'd better get started on that soup. It's a little harder up here to make it than at home."

"Are you from Phoenix?"

"Dallas. I come to this cabin every fall and spring, if possible." She crossed to the fireplace, squatted by the logs and began to build a fire. It would be cold once the sun set, so even if she weren't going to fix soup, she would've made a fire to keep them warm.

"Why? This isn't the Ritz."

"I like to get totally away from civilization."

"You've succeeded."

"Why were you hiking up here? Do you have a campsite nearby? Maybe someone's looking for you—someone I can search for tomorrow." Once the fire started going, she found the iron pot and slipped it on the hook that would swing over the blaze.

"No, I came alone. I like to get away from it all, too. Take photographs."

"Where's your camera?" Where's your wallet and your driver's license?

"It's all still fuzzy. I think my backpack with my satellite phone and camera went over the cliff when I fell. A ledge broke my fall."

He'd fallen from a cliff? That explanation sent all her alarms blaring. Tess filled the pot with purified water from the container she'd stocked yesterday and dumped some chicken noodle soup from a packet into it. "How did you get shot?" she asked, glancing back to make sure he was awake.

His dark eyebrows slashed downward. "I'm not sure. I think a hunter mistook me for a deer."

"A deer?" Not likely.

"I saw two hunters earlier yesterday. One minute I was standing near a cliff enjoying the gorgeous view of the sunset, the next minute..." His frown deepened. "I woke up on a ledge a few feet from the cliff I had been standing on, so I guess I fell over the edge. It was getting dark, but I could still see the blood on the rock where I must have hit my head and my leg felt on fire."

"You dragged yourself up from the ledge and somehow made it here?"

"Yes."

She whistled. "You're mighty determined."

"I have a teenage daughter at home. I'm a single dad. I had no choice." Determination glinted in his eyes, almost persuading her he was telling the truth. But what if it was all a lie? She couldn't risk believing him without proof. For all she knew, he was a criminal, and she was in danger.

"Okay, so you think a hunter mistakenly shot you. Are you sure about that? Why would he leave you to die?"

"Maybe he didn't realize what he'd done? Maybe his shot ricocheted off the rock and hit me? I don't know." He scrubbed his hand across his forehead. "What other explanation would there be?"

You're lying to me. She couldn't shake the thought.

"Someone wanted to kill you."

About the Author

USA Today Bestselling author, Margaret Daley, is multi-published with over 100 titles and 5 million books sold worldwide. She had written for Harlequin, Abingdon, Kensington, Dell, and Simon and Schuster. She has won multiple awards, including the prestigious Carol Award, Holt Medallion and Inspirational Readers' Choice Contest.

She has been married for over forty-five years and is enjoying being a grandma. When she isn't traveling, she's writing love stories, often with a suspense thread and corralling her three cats that think they rule her household. To find out more about Margaret visit her website at www.margaretdaley.com.

Made in the USA
Middletown, DE
05 February 2022

60592200R00152